ALSO BY KATE JENNINGS

POETRY
Come to Me, My Melancholy Baby
Mother I'm Rooted (editor)
Cats, Dogs & Pitchforks

STORIES
Women Falling Down in the Street

NOVELS
Snake

ESSAYS
Save Me, Joe Louis
Bad Manners

A Division of HarperCollins*Publishers*

Moral Hazard

A NOVEL

Kate Jennings

FOURTH ESTATE · *London* and *New York*

HarperCollins books may be purchased for educational,
business, or sales promotional use. For information, please write:
Special Markets Department, HarperCollins Publishers Inc.,
10 East 53rd Street, New York, NY 10022.

FIRST EDITION

Designed by Dinah Drazin

Printed on acid-free paper

Library of Congress Cataloging-in-Publication Data

Jennings, Kate.
    Moral hazard: a novel/Kate Jennings. – 1st ed.
        p. cm.
    ISBN 0–00–714108–4 (hc : acid-free paper)
    1. Women speechwriters—Fiction. 2. Alzheimer's disease—
Patients—Fiction. 3. Women in finance—Fiction. 4. New York
(N.Y.)—Fiction. 5. Married women—Fiction. 6. Wall Street—
Fiction. I. Title.

    PR9619.3.J44 M67 2002
    823'.914—dc21   2002019926

Bob Cato

1923–1999

he sang his didn't he danced his did

Moral Hazard

1

How would you have me write about it? Bloody awful, all of it.

I will tell my story as straight as I can, as straight as anyone's crooked recollections allow. I will tell it in my own voice, although treating myself as another, observed, appeals. If I can, no jokes or jibes, no persiflage—my preferred defenses. I'd rather eat garden worms than be earnest or serious. Or sentimental.

I recount the events of those years with great reluctance. Not because you might think less of me—there is always that. No, the reason is a rule I try to follow, summed up by Ellen Burstyn in the movie *Alice Doesn't Live Here Anymore*: "Don't look back. You'll turn into a pillar of shit."

See? I can't help it. Wisecracking—a reflex. I've lived in New York for several decades, but I was born

in Australia, where the fine art of undercutting ourselves—and others—is learned along with our ABCs.
Australians—clowns, debunkers.

I have to start somewhere, so it might as well be
with Mike.

2

I met Mike—beanpole Mike, angular and awkward as Abe Lincoln and looking a little like him—in Pasqua, a coffee shop in the World Financial Center, downtown in Battery Park City. Long gone, replaced by a Starbucks, Pasqua was popular with the bankers, traders, analysts, lawyers, and back-office types who worked in the center's towers because the coffee was heavy, viscous, bitter—a powerful propellant. Not to be trifled with. Drink enough Pasqua coffee and you were *orbiting*.

Mike was standing behind me in the impatient, early morning line that tailed out the door. I ordered a large black, and he said, speaking over my shoulder to the young man behind the counter, "Same for me," to save time.

"Diesel fuel," I said, conversationally, but staring

ahead, as New Yorkers do, so as not to be intrusive.

"Liquid amphetamine," he replied.

Amphetamine? The phrase "amphetamine activists," from the sixties, somehow emerged from the recesses of my mind. I sneaked a look at him, taking in his large nose and tufty hair and thought, *My age, ugly as an eagle*. I faced the counter again.

Through the window, across the damp plaza, last passengers were leaking from the Jersey ferry, heads bent against the puncturing cold, coats buttoned, scarves wound tight, gloved hands holding bags and briefcases or thrust into pockets. The Hudson was in a bleak mood, turned in on itself, indifferent, with scraps of ice bunched at the edge, driven there by the current.

Our paths crossed again several days later because, as it turned out, we both worked for Niedecker Benecke, the investment bank. You will know it: not quite top tier but bumping against Goldman Sachs, Merrill Lynch, and Morgan Stanley. At the time—the winter of 1993–1994—financial services companies were shrugging off the recession induced by the excesses of the eighties and ramping up for the excesses of the nineties. Corporate raiders and junk-bond peddlers—Mike Milken, Ivan Boesky, Carl Icahn—were the past. Joseph Jett, Nick Leeson, the Asian meltdown, CNBC, irrational exuberance, the 10,000 Dow, the dot-com boom—that was to be the future. As was the dot-com bust, the obliteration of the World Trade Center, recession, fear. Dragon's teeth sown.

I was writing a speech on derivatives for Niedecker's general counsel to be given at a gathering of an international regulatory body in Japan. Hellishly complicated, computer-generated financial contracts, derivatives are the brainchildren of those math pointy-heads known, in Wall Street lingo, as "quants"—from the word "quantum," I'd guess. Derivatives and the regulation of them were particularly contentious in the early nineties, although, as one old-timer commodities trader told me, sniffily, they'd been around, in one form or other, since the Sumerians. "Once upon a time, it was commodities, then futures, now derivatives," he'd opined, delicately shooting his cuffs. "It's all structured finance. It's all aimed at neutralizing risk by parceling it up, selling it to someone else. Quanting around, nothing new in that."

The general counsel ordered me to research views

within Niedecker on derivatives, including those of the head of the risk-management unit. That was Mike. A math pointy-head himself, he had the job, in part, of monitoring the activities of the firm's quants. Heaven knows, nobody else in executive management had a clue what they were up to.

I knocked on the frame of his open door. "We have a two-thirty." In true corporate fashion, I was left to flap on the threshold, drying, waiting for him to acknowledge me. An interminable minute passed. Mike took a last look at the screen of his computer and in a single, abrupt movement was at the door, hand extended.

"I remember you. The coffee shop."

"Yes."

"You're from Communications, right? A speech for——?" He named the general counsel, famous among unyielding men for being unyielding. "Writing for him, huh? What did you do wrong?" Laughed, high up, in his nose.

I explained the speech, switched on my tape recorder, and asked my dutiful questions. We covered the Group of Thirty recommendations for derivatives regulation, the GAO response, the Basle Agreement.

He gave the standard financial industry arguments. Derivatives are risk-management tools, nothing but beneficial, a boon to investors and the economy. To regulate them would be to hinder the flow of money, disrupt the global good. Et cetera.

Mike's answers were peculiarly without enthusiasm. For the most part, when Communications personnel come calling, corporate henchmen are all smiles: upbeat, encouraging, patient. And no doubt sigh with relief once we are out of sight. One can never be too careful.

Mike was unusual in another respect: he didn't use jargon or clichés. Agent Orange words. "Liquidity" and "transparency," yes, but not "going forward," "pro-active," "paradigm," "incentivize," "added value," "comfort level," "outside the box," "a rising tide lifts all boats." He didn't even use "fungible," a word that was enjoying a big vogue. So I ventured a last, offhand question. "What do you *really* think of derivatives?" Worth a try.

He quickened. "The mathematics can be awesome. You have to *admire* the mathematics. And they *can* be an excellent risk-management tool . . ." He trailed off, obviously wondering whether he should continue.

"Well, it helps to look at derivatives like atoms. Split them one way and you have heat and energy—useful stuff. Split them another way, and you have a bomb. You have to understand the subtleties."

Understand the subtleties. God is in the details. Cracks me up.

3

Cath. That's my name. At the time of the events I am recounting, I was in my forties: bedrock feminist, unreconstructed left-winger, with literary tastes that ran to recherché writers like Charlotte Mew and Ivy Compton-Burnett. You will perhaps know of Charlotte Mew: a melancholic Georgian poet who, beset by financial problems and bouts of insanity, drank a bottle of lysol. Dame Ivy—peer of Henry Green, Sylvia Townsend-Warner, and Molly Keane, immediate ancestor of Muriel Spark—wrote abrupt, conversational novels about small cruelties and how power, even in minute amounts, can be abused.

Ivy, Henry, Sylvia, Molly, Muriel: they assumed intelligence—emotional as well as intellectual—on the part of the reader. I shouldn't write of Muriel Spark in the past tense, but she is no different from the others, grievously neglected, well on her way to being reduced to marginalia, cult status.

I digress, although it amuses me to see an old passion flicker to life. I was attempting to describe myself. Not my physical appearance—you can imagine that for yourself—but my beliefs. Opinions. Prejudices. These, formed by the politics of the sixties and firmly held, were not so much unexamined as untested.

You can guess them: affirmative action, a woman's right to choose, a judicious redistribution of wealth, parity for everyone in all things. I was against the obvious: capital punishment, egregious pollution, trickle-down economics. Absurd exercise, I know. I might as well say I am for ice cream and against monogrammed hand towels. *You* write down your beliefs without sounding pompous.

Another try. I was for civility and a sense of humor, against anyone who had stopped listening, receiving, changing. People who had no *give*. Of course, I disapproved of bankers, on principle. Not that I knew any. Until this job, I had worked and made friends with people who shared my views. Mostly moral, mostly kind.

An unlikely candidate, then, for the job of executive

speechwriter, to be putting words in the mouths of plutocrats deeply suspicious of metaphors and words of more than two syllables. "SAT word!" "$10 word!" they would write in the margins of draft speeches. There were some inexplicable exceptions, such as the aforementioned "fungible" or, a more recent example, "granular," which, having gained acceptance against all odds, were clutched as tenaciously as a child might a favorite toy.

An unlikely candidate, too, to be working for a firm whose culture had been shaped by the kind of drive required to shave dimes off dollars without actually making something useful or entertaining, something that could be touched or enjoyed. A firm whose ethic was borrowed in equal parts from the Marines, the CIA, and Las Vegas. A firm where women were about as welcome as fleas in a sleeping bag.

But you are meeting me at a time when my judgment was suspended, my tastes in literature, or anything else, for that matter, irrelevant. I didn't have the luxury. The reason was my husband, Bailey.

After a youth entirely lacking in forethought, I had married. Married? Bedrock feminist? It happens. Sweet Bailey, dearest Bailey. Twenty-five years older than me, imprudent as I, but who cared? He was optimistic where I was pessimistic; enthusiastic where I was distrustful; charming, outgoing, where I was withdrawn, intense. He saw the point of me, not always discernible, and I would have loved him for that alone. He was always doing, always curious. He surrounded me with warmth.

I haven't put on rose-tinted glasses. We had our problems. George Eliot once wrote that marriage is awful in its nearness. I agree. Yoked together, *bound*, in a three-legged race with no finishing line.

We lived on the Upper East Side in an apartment with milky north light, where the noise of traffic was dim, muffled, and we were happy beyond expectation. When the nearness, the three-legged race, got too much for me, I took off for a week or two, to write a travel story, do a profile, whatever.

Bailey earned his living as a designer—books, magazines, CDs, posters—but he was also a collagist. He'd had shows of his collages over the years, but his work was not impersonal enough to make him a ranking artist, a contender. It was too engaging, too emotional. All of Bailey, his every idiosyncrasy, was in his collages.

We had ten good years. Marvelous years. Then, he

began forgetting. This was not immediately obvious to anyone but me because Bailey was expert in covering his lapses. He skimmed over them like a water-strider. Neurologists, I later learned, call this being "well defended." Worse, his judgment became poor and his business sense, not good at the best of times, turned disastrous. His perception of the world splintering, his horizons warping, he became frustrated, scared, angry. He raged, pounded walls, accused me of all kinds of perfidy. This, the most trusting and uxorious of men.

I will spare you the round of doctors we saw over the next two years. The very first, a neurologist, had known what it was: Alzheimer's. He was reluctant to venture a diagnosis because it was too early and he had no definite way, except by elimination of other illnesses, of determining the disease. But when we returned to him, at the beginning of a long winter, he suggested, in addition to a battery of cognitive testing, a new procedure: a spinal tap to measure the levels of the protein that causes neurons to gum up, to knot and tangle, obliterating memory, undoing everything learned.

In the waiting room, before the doctor gave us the

final report, I sat hugging my overcoat while Bailey watched horrified as a thin, gray-haired, dapper man with a walking stick went around introducing himself to all and sundry, courteous, bobbing his head, smiling hugely, like a celebrity in front of photographers. When he finished his circuit, he started all over again.

"Oh God," said Bailey, "don't ever let me get like that."

Bailey's amyloid-beta protein level was through the roof. So sad, such a shame, especially for a vital man, said the neurologist, after he had dispatched Bailey to the examination room. Leaning back in his chair, fiddling with his fountain pen, surrounded by teetering files and potted phalaenopsids, gifts from grateful patients, he added, "You will have to say good-bye to the man you love." Normally I might have asked if he wasn't being unnecessarily melodramatic, but I had been catapulted into shock, the rush of air displacing my thoughts, my emotions. I sat mute.

Do you know the Irish song that goes something like this? *Maids, when you are young/Never wed an old man.*

4

I asked Bailey what the doctor had said. "A small part of my brain has gone wrong, and he'll fix it," he replied.

A deep breath. "That's not what he said at all." And I repeated the doctor's words.

You will think me cruel. I could have lied, gone along with the delusion, but my role in our marriage had always been to bring Bailey back to earth, be his ballast. Left to himself, Bailey became airborne with notions and grand plans. He flew in the face of facts. By sheer will, by wanting something to be so, he would *prevail*.

I cried for five days straight, until my eyes were swollen shut. A bill arrived from the doctor, and in the space provided for the diagnosis was written *dementia*. Pretty word, end-of-the-world word. The vocabulary of senility. Other words and phrases came to mind: *gaga, away with the pixies, lost his marbles, nobody home*. Knowing next to nothing about Alzheimer's other than these cruel, dismissive tags, I went to Barnes and Noble on Eighty-sixth Street, pulled out all the books on the disease, and, sitting on one of those round rubber step stools, worked my way through them, hysteria rising until I thought it would gush from me, gouts of it, like water from a fire hydrant.

I learned the obvious: Without memory, we are nothing. I also learned that the disease wasn't a slow slide, a long good-bye into nothingness, but more like descending in a malfunctioning, bumpy elevator into something approximating childhood. A childhood imagined by Goya or Buñuel. Or George Romero. Bailey would lose not just his memory of events and people but all his skills, from the most sophisticated to the elementary—from language to control over his bodily functions. He would forget how to swallow, walk backward when he wanted to go forward, become sexually "inappropriate." Maybe not all of those things—the disease affects people differently, some pacing and cursing as if the hounds of hell were after them, others sinking into immobility and sweetness—but he would, as they all do, forget to remember. Bailey would erode like a sandstone statue, becoming formless and vague, reduced to a nub. This would take, oh, about seven years.

5

A Greyhound bus out of town. Be gone. That would be an answer. After it was all over, in the middle of another winter, exhausted, cold to my bones, colder still in my heart, I thought about Greyhound buses again, buses heading to warm weather, to Miami, but worried that I would die, like Ratso in *Midnight Cowboy*, before I got there, in my own spreading puddle of pee.

The doctor suggested I join a group for Alzheimer's caregivers that a social worker from his neurology unit had started. ("Caretaker"—of a human shell—is more apt.) The day of the first meeting it snowed, and the streets filled with slush. Only two other women— dignified, Jewish, in their sixties—attended. We pulled our chairs up to a round table that was too big for so few, and the social worker asked if anything in particular was worrying us. We all shook our heads. To get the discussion going, she broached the subject of sex, although she referred to it as "intimacy." The house of illness is papered with euphemisms.

The first woman said, "He is my husband. He will always be my husband."

The second woman chewed on her lip, crumbled. "I can't. He would like me to, but I can't." She started to cry, then gathered herself to say, "You know what I hate? When I'm dressing him, he holds his arms up so I can pull on his sweater. Just like a child." She thrust her hands in the air to demonstrate. "I—don't—want—a—child," she said, hawking up the words, making them gobs of disgust.

Attention shifted to me. I tried to retract my head into my body. A secretary knocked on the door, summoning the social worker to a phone call. While she was gone, the three of us attempted to chat.

"How long has your husband had Alzheimer's?" one asked.

"Early days," I said. "Only just diagnosed."
Silence.

"I can't bear this," I blurted. "You're describing our future."

"You shouldn't be here. Not yet. Come later, when he's more advanced."

And the two of them, on my behalf, ganged up on the social worker when she returned, telling her that the group wasn't right for me.

The social worker at the second group I tried, at the Alzheimer's Association, was as condescending in her cheerfulness as the other had been in her gravity. (Social workers are damned if they do, damned if they don't.) This time we sat in a circle on metal chairs in a dun-colored room, no table, exposed as pigeons.

A woman my age spoke first. Both her parents had Alzheimer's. Both? Oh sweet Jesus. After forty years of marriage, her parents, this husband and wife, were strangers to each other. The wife spent her days trying to evict her husband from the house; the husband was trying to do the same to her. In moments of rare lucidity, they joined forces and turned on their live-in home-care worker, to have *her* evicted.

Another woman—diffident, proud, African American, in her seventies—spoke up. She was the caregiver for her sister. The two of them had always made a fuss of birthdays, but now her sister couldn't grasp the idea of a birthday, much less celebrate one. "What *is* the point?" the woman wanted to know, not sad or resigned but furled with anger. "What *is* the point?"

During this time, Bailey was seemingly undisturbed, except when asleep, and then he clawed the air and shouted unintelligible words, desperate as someone buried alive. I would wake him, hold him, until he calmed down. He'd tell me how he didn't want to die, not yet, not when he had so much work to do, not now that he had me and his life had finally fallen into place. Have I told you how much I loved him? Bailey: my family.

In his waking hours, chuckling to himself, Bailey started designing a magazine for Alzheimer's patients. It would include a profile of Alois Alzheimer, an interview with Nancy Reagan, spreads of the later paintings of Willem de Kooning. When that idea lost its appeal, he took out large sheets of drawing paper and began, for the last time, remembering his generous, eventful life. Now, while he worked, he cried. He cried for a year, his face bruising with sorrow.

Disease is expensive, beyond the means of a freelance writer. So I began canvassing all our powerful friends and acquaintances, one of whom had a connection to Niedecker. He nixed the obvious field, publishing, saying that I was going to need serious money. He made some phone calls, and that is how I came to be in an office in a downtown Manhattan tower, wearing a hastily purchased suit and binding pantyhose, struggling with the intricacies of finance and corporate hierarchy, learning to put on faces and be excessively deferential. Ruth among the alien corn.

The year before, Bailey had made a prescient charcoal drawing depicting a wizened man contemplating Lady Death. Underneath, in his graceful script: *There are times at their very beginnings when you wish for their end.*

6

That first summer of Bailey's disease, when I left the apartment building for work, against all reason, I felt life had possibilities. For a brief moment, after I said good-morning to Ronnie, next to the elevator, and Henry, at the front door, both blank-eyed and bored in the way of doormen conserving their energy better to stoke their grievances, I had spring in my step.

The pavement was always freshly hosed, thin puddles on the concrete, cool air against my skin. The dog-owners from our building were abroad: Carmen with his bulldog, Buddha; Marge with her pug, Peaches. Carmen was dark, good-looking, funny. Buddha is a farm animal, he liked to say, all he does is eat and shit, which didn't stop Carmen from taking Buddha to the vet in the middle of the night with bull-dog ailments, leaving him more ragged than parents of a one-month-old. Marge was surreptitiously smoking. Her husband had died from emphysema, hence the surreptitiousness, although it was not smoking but eating that would do Marge in. Peaches was as fat as her owner and waddled like Buddha.

At the corner of Lexington Avenue, I joined a trickle of people with determined strides making for the Hunter College subway station. There, the trickle became a stream; at Grand Central, a tributary. Possibilities quickly evaporated in the fetid underground air and jigsaw of bodies. Some read copies of the *Times* folded with origami precision or pushed their noses into chunky paperbacks, as if afflicted with acute near-sightedness. Others listened to Walkmans, nodding in tune and lip-synching. I closed my eyes and breathed shallowly, the better to ignore the heat and the proximity of strangers. Only seven-thirty in the morning and already the cloth of my blouse stuck to my skin. Only seven-thirty in the morning and already I was on my toes, wary, ready to go on the offensive at the slightest provocation.

At the Fulton Street subway stop, a press of people oozed like molasses through the turnstiles and up the narrow stairways. Expelled into air twenty degrees cooler, I shook myself to regain my composure, un-stuck my blouse from my back. A huddle of shoppers was already waiting for Century 21 to open its doors. I gladly would have joined them if anxiety about the day's work were not beginning to tie my stomach in knots. The store's haphazardness and lack of polish made it a cult favorite with shoppers. It didn't run to air-conditioning or even dressing rooms, so patrons sportingly stripped in the aisles. In a section marked EUROPEAN FASHIONS, indicated as such by a scrib-bled sign tacked to a wall with tape, the more outré and unsellable of last year's Gaultier and Versace could be found, as every French tourist and drag queen worth their salt knew. Slapping the racks at Century 21 was like being let loose in a costume museum.

I headed across the World Trade Center plaza, skirting the towers, slowing my steps to crane at their immoderate height and listen to the keening that flowed down the fluted aluminum facade. The gods, I liked to imagine, bemoaning the hubris they saw in the pokey skyscrapers, dog-leg streets, and chewing gum-stained sidewalks of New York's unprepossess-ing financial district. Then over to West Street, on the walkway, a moment of unease at the sight of workers below repairing the damage from the 1993 terrorist bomb blast, to the World Financial Center, built on landfill from the World Trade Center and occupied, along with Niedecker, by American Express, Merrill Lynch, Nomura, Deloitte & Touche, and Dow Jones. The walkway deposited pedestrians in the Winter Garden, an awkward atrium housing palm trees: Trader Vic's on a grand scale. Through the Winter Garden, a stop for coffee, to Hanny.

Hanny. My boss. My *manager*.

No matter how early I arrived at work, Hanny was already at his desk. He sometimes slept under it or at least on the couch opposite, I'd deduced from his rumpled clothes, rather than go home to Connecticut, where he had an unaccommodating wife, as he'd wasted no time telling me. Hanny was unfortunate not just in his wife but also in his name, which was short for Hannibal. Some joked that he should be treated like Hannibal Lecter and locked up, with speeches slipped through the bars. And then there was his appearance, regrettably toadlike: pudgy, with wide-apart eyes, flat lips that stretched almost from ear to ear, and skin that patched with perspiration at the slightest exertion.

Hanny was not only at his desk but waiting for an audience in order to relieve himself of opinions provoked by the morning's newspapers. He was an enthusiastic bigot. The predictable groups got him steamed—blacks, feminists, homosexuals—but his special ire was reserved, strangely, for the disabled. Or, to be more accurate, the Americans with Disabilities Act, which was costing businesses and taxpayers "billions."

On my first day at the job, Hanny had leaned in close—he was true to type in every respect—to impart some wisdom. "I hear you are a bohemian, a left-winger." He didn't wait for an answer. "You'll become conservative working here. You wait and see. Everyone does." Then he handed me a book he had at the ready. It was Robert Bartley's *The Seven Fat Years*. I hadn't known who Bartley was: the notoriously conservative editor of the *Wall Street Journal*'s op-ed page. His book was an account of the supposed munificence that had flowed from Reagan-era economics. Bartley was one of Hanny's gods, along with Reagan, of course, and Margaret Thatcher. Lined up on the other side were Bill Clinton—"despicable"—and Ralph Nader—"an instrument of the devil."

(Democrats had yet to come to this same viewpoint about Nader, after the 2000 election.) I later learned that he gave this book to anyone under his tutelage. Eager to please, I read the book overnight and returned it, saying, "I don't like true believers of any stripe," a comment that whizzed right by him, a tiny meteor missing earth's dense bulk and continuing into outer space.

Hanny's knowledge of finance was only as deep as it needed to be and sometimes verged on the fantastic, but he produced corporate propaganda with the efficiency of a sausage machine. He was different from most hacks in that he believed what he wrote. In fact, he saw himself as the repository of the firm's values—"touchstones"—because the apex of his career had been to give voice to them. His bromides were not only published in an expensive booklet, to be distributed to new recruits, but also engraved on brass plates attached to walls, chiseled into marble floors, pressed into Lucite paperweights. The words "respect" and "integrity" figured large.

As time went by and I became aware of the anthill of lawyers on the company payroll defending the firm against lapses in the very values that Hanny described,

I stupidly wondered aloud in his company whether they really were coded into the firm's DNA, as we so often wrote in speeches. If you have to make a fuss of moral fiber, you probably lack it, et cetera. In his rectitude, Hanny reared up. "The touchstones are *aspirational*. In any company, there are peaks and there are troughs. It's our job to describe the peaks."

His voice, adenoidal and Midwestern, could be obsequious one moment, vicious the next. Obsequious with his bosses—Hanny was proud of his ability to "manage up"—and vicious with his staff. After an editing session with him—he called it "tweaking" or "word-smithing"—we all left his office sniffling or red-faced. The problem was not that the speeches, letters, and other miscellany that were our province had to arrive on Hanny's superiors' desks on time, pitch-perfect, no typos. That went without saying. It was that they had to be exactly as he conceived them. As a result, we spent most of our time trying to get into Hanny's head, not the happiest of places. We needn't have bothered. He always moved the goalposts.

Hanny peppered his conversation with phrases like "rat's ass" and "slicker than greased goose shit." If you were late with a speech because you'd just had your leg amputated and thought that the executive would understand, Hanny might say, "He doesn't give a rat's ass about you. All he wants is the speech on his desk." And he was right. As for the latter, improbable as it seems, Hanny used it as a term of praise. He admired people who were slicker than greased goose shit and aspired to be that way himself.

I had quite a crew above me—up the chain— at Niedecker. Above Hanny, for example, was Bart, who feigned aggression like a barracuda, flaring his features and daring you to come any closer. He was known for appearing suddenly out of his office and yelling orders, whether anyone was there to listen or not. Every now and again, he crossed the line and was sent off to what us bottom-feeders called "charm school"—managerial training sessions. Hanny crossed the line all the time but was not as visible as Bart, who ran the press group. A flack as opposed to a hack.

Above Hanny, above Bart, was Chuck. The head of our department, Chuck had been a college basket-ball player, an all-American golden boy. His alley-oop glory days were still discernible underneath encroaching flab and adult worries, like pentimento in a painting. He lived to please, loved to schmooze. Heads of Communications keep their positions by either knowing where the bodies are buried or jumping in the laps of executives and licking their faces. Chuck did a bit of both. Whatever might be said of him, he was expert at placating our senior executives, at whose pleasure we served. He was hard to dislike, even if he managed his department by hiring people with ingrown personalities like Hanny and Bart and letting them loose.

This, of course, was the stuff of Dilbert or *New Yorker* cartoons. But it wasn't funny, not living it. Hanny and Bart seemed to me as sadistic as prefects at an English boarding school. As a result, the path from our group to the company psychiatrist was well trodden. Only one of us—a woman from New Jersey who cheerfully referred to herself as a Polack and who supervised the production of brochures—was immune. "What do they think I am? Chopped liver?" she'd say, laughing with her entire body and picking up the phone to resume her talkathon with her vast network of Niedecker pals. When I asked her how she remained sanguine, she said, "Hey. I've seen a lot of Hannys and Barts come and go."

Our group was not unique. I had gained a whole different view of New York's skyscrapers. I looked at them and didn't see architecture. I saw infestations of middle managers, tortuous chains of command, stupor-inducing meetings, ever-widening gyres of e-mail. I saw people scratching up dust like chickens and calling it work. I saw the devil whooping it up.

To find my way, I asked questions. In their eyes, I questioned. I probably did that, too, but more out of naiveté and, I must admit, incredulity. In the normal course, I would have been expelled immediately for the foreign organism that I was, but I had a "connection," so instead was labeled "high maintenance" and ignored, with the occasional attempt, in the form of team reviews and dressings-down, to re-educate me. After one review, Hanny informed me with absolute seriousness that my sense of humor was such that people thought I wasn't taking the job seriously. Dear reader, with effort, I kept a straight face. Another time, he told me I was their diversity challenge: age, gender, nationality, lack of corporate experience. Shades of the Cultural Revolution.

In time, I settled for an anthropological approach. I was in the belly of the beast: observe, listen, learn.

After all, the job was serving its purpose. There was money for the rent and to buy Cognex, the new Alzheimer's drug. Not only that, to survive the quicksand at Niedecker, I had to give the job my full attention, leaving me less time to dwell on Bailey.

That first summer, after work, I took to wandering the aisles of Century 21, not shopping, only relieved to be where nothing was demanded of me. I was commuting, it seemed, between two forms of dementia, two circles of hell. Neither point nor meaning to Alzheimer's, nor to corporate life, unless you counted the creation of shareholder value.

That first summer, once or twice, instead of worming my way uptown on the Number 5 subway, I splurged on a taxi home. The route was along the FDR Drive, by the shouldering waters of the East River, its bridges and their mastodonic spans, by the Lower East Side playing fields and their antiquated stadium lighting banked in uneven clusters and resembling graying dowager diamonds. If the traffic allowed, and the rattle of the straining taxi ignored, you had the illusion of swooping, soaring, above the clogged confusion of the city.

That first summer, when I came home, Bailey was

always to be found sitting immediately inside the door, waiting for me, our cat in his arms, both alert to my arrival.

That first summer, after Bailey was asleep, I lay on the sofa in the living room, watching the shifting evening sky above the Carlyle Hotel and listening to musicals: *South Pacific, Carousel, Kismet, The King and I.* I fell in love with the voices of William Tabbert and Alfred Drake, with music that consoled in its hopefulness. Music that was as far from my circumstances as could be imagined. *Play on the cymbal, the timbale, the lyre/Play with appropriate passion, fashion/Songs of delight and delicious desire . . .*

7

The anthropological approach to corporate life was Mike's idea; I was too off-balance, too thrown by events, to think of it. Mike and I became friends on the day of Nixon's funeral, declared a holiday on Wall Street. Hanny hadn't taken the day off—a big speech was pressing—so neither did I. As usual, the first item on my agenda was to be Hanny's audience. Naturally, he went into raptures about Nixon: a *great* man.

Escaping, I went down to the front of the World Financial Center, where pink granite benches face a marina. One of these achieved notoriety when a trader sat down and calmly shot himself on a sunny day, people promenading, seagulls perching, boats plowing. Mike arrived shortly after I did and settled on the same bench.

"Hello," I said. Forward of me. Though we'd met a couple of times, I didn't expect him to remember me. After all, he was executive management, and I a dime-a-dozen vice president.

"Hi." He slid a little closer. "If I remember, you're Cath. The derivatives speech. How'd it go?"

"It went fine."

Mike was a smoker and so was I. Mike, I found out, had never bothered to give it up. I had stopped years ago, but with Bailey's illness, resumed, telling myself, whatever gets you through the night. I took painkillers, for migraines, and too many of them, no doubt. I was probably ripe for an intervention. The idea of anyone willingly intervening in my life made me laugh out loud, and still does. Husband with Alzheimer's? He's all yours, gal.

We lit up, sipped coffee. Mike broke the silence. "'The Day Lady Died.' That's my favorite O'Hara poem." This was not out of the blue. Marvelously, some lines of Frank O'Hara wind along the wrought-iron fence that fronts the marina:

One need never leave the confines of New York
to get all the greenery one wishes—I can't even

enjoy a blade of grass unless I know there's a
subway handy, or a record store or some other
sign that people do not totally regret life.

Walt Whitman is there, too:

City of the world. (For all races are here, all the
lands of the earth make contributions here.) City
of the sea! City of the wharves and stores—city
of the tall facades of marble and iron! Proud and
passionate city—mettlesome, mad, extravagant
city!

So Mike knew his O'Hara. And that is how our friendship began. A New York friendship, given it was
restricted to the bench and the conversations we had
there; like a Greek drama, all the action was off-stage.
A friendship larded with the cultural allusions and
references common to people of our age, background,
education.

"Not taking the day off?" I ventured, unsure where
to go with O'Hara.

"For Nixon? No. Definitely no." His turn to take the
conversation in another direction. "How long have you
worked for Niedecker?"

"A year."

"Before that?"

"I was a freelancer. Magazines. Travel stories, pro-
files, some essays, that kind of stuff. Never worked in
finance. Totally new to it." I told him about Bailey.

"So sorry." A few more slow drags. It was a cool,
windy day, with streaky clouds. Because of the wind,
Mike was smoking like James Dean, his cigarette
hooded by his hand. Anyone less like James Dean than
Mike—large head, bony body that he occupied as if it
were rented—I couldn't imagine. "What do you make
of it, then?" coughing as he asked and gesturing at the
towers behind us, at Niedecker.

"The finance part is falling into place. It's like a
foreign language. Immerse yourself and it begins
to make sense. But the corporate side. Jeepers. That's
much harder. And the guys I work for—holy cow. I'm
realizing I've led a sheltered life." Mike laughed.

Several days before, I was directed to talk to Bart
about a group of Chinese sponsored by Niedecker
to visit the United States to study the financial
markets. He had done more than warm to his subject.
Apoplectic, he'd barked, "Goddamn communists! I
don't know why we're helping them." I related this

and moved on to Hanny and his tirades. If Mike knew his O'Hara and wasn't enthralled with Nixon, I figured I was on safe ground.

"Poorly socialized," he said. "But at least you know where you stand with them."

"True. But . . ." Agitated. His observation hadn't seemed sufficient. I was about to say something to that effect when Mike interrupted.

"Can I give you some advice?"

"Okay." Feeling small.

"That's not going to change." Gesturing behind us, again. "And those guys aren't going to change. If you keep throwing yourself against Niedecker, against them, you'll break into a million pieces. Round off your sharp edges. Turn yourself into an anthropologist."

"A naturalist with an ant colony."

"That's the spirit. You know, Wall Street isn't as bad as it seems. Sure, it gets its share of bigots and silver-spoon types. That's the downside. But it also tolerates eccentrics who wouldn't find employment anywhere else. You'd be surprised. At one time, having a short attention span was the *only* qualification you needed to work down here." His peculiar nasal laugh. "It's not quite that way now. The dead hand of Human

Resources homogenizing everything." He broke off to light another cigarette. "I know one guy, a trader, who's an anarchist and proud of it. But nobody cares because he's good at his job. And then there're people like you and me."

"You?" Offhand. As if I weren't dying to know.

In the clipped cadences of the busy Wall Streeter, he gave me his history. "Columbia, majored in mathematics. Joined SDS. The antiwar organization." A glance my way. "Don't look so surprised."

A rabble-rouser from the sixties running the risk management unit at Niedecker? I was surprised, but it was no more improbable than my writing speeches for its executives. Actually, I was tickled. I'd done time on the barricades myself.

"Harvard for postdoc studies," continued Mike. "Hot bed for quants. Steve Ross was there. Also a radical. Or at least he was then. Marx turned him onto economics, finance. Same here." Another glance to gauge my reaction. "We're not the first to arrive on the Street via the Moor, although nobody is going to admit it." The Moor. My oh my. Marx's children's nickname for their father. This was unreal.

Silence. "After Harvard, a stint at J. P. Morgan.

Boring bunch. Heads up butts, minds in neutral. And then Niedecker. It's been fifteen years." Another glance. "You don't know who Steve Ross is, do you?"

I shook my head.

"Option pricing trees. Brilliant guy." He paused. "You've probably read Adam Smith, Keynes, maybe some Galbraith, not much else, right?"

"Right."

"I'll send you a couple of books."

"Thanks."

"Gotta go," said Mike, stubbing out his second cigarette.

"Me too."

We walked together to the Winter Garden, passing other smokers, some in groups, some solitary. The promised books arrived in the internal mail the next day, and my education in modern finance began.

8

We had gone through the nightly routine.

First, a Stouffer's frozen dinner, the extent of my cooking abilities. In the good years, Bailey always cooked for us. For him, food was a ceremony; even if he were eating by himself, he set the table as if for a special event. But cloves had wound up in the pepper grinder, plastic wrapping left on meat, a kitchen towel placed on a burner. He gave it up voluntarily, as he was giving up everything, redrawing his boundaries in order to preserve his dignity, but keeping an illusion of activity.

Then we watched the evening news, which included a segment on the newest hope for people with Alzheimer's. These segments ran, cruelly, at least once a week. They still do. Current advice to prevent Alzheimer's: Eat leafy green vegetables. At that time, though, they mostly involved the results of a study of Canadian nuns. The better educated the nun, the more she exercised her brain, a researcher had concluded, the less likely she would be to develop Alzheimer's. This was the opposite view of the home healthcare workers I chatted with in the elevator of our apartment building. Jamaican and Filipino women with reserves of compassion, they believed that Alzheimer's was the result of overworking the brain, no doubt because the people they cared for had the money to hire them, entailing education, careers.

That night, the segment was about the development of genetically engineered, memory-impaired mice. It was billed as a major breakthrough. I always watched these segments with hope pricking in me—hope that turned to blasphemous fury when "the latest best new hope for Alzheimer's sufferers" turned out to be insulting generalizations derived from small and unrepresentative populations, or scientific breakthroughs that would yield real results in twenty years' time. "Fucking nuns," I'd say, out of Bailey's earshot. That night: "Fucking mice."

Next, coaxing him out of his clothes and under the shower. Once a fastidious man, vain about his appearance, he would come to bed fully dressed and unwashed if I let him. The business of bathing was too complex for him, the feel of water alien on his skin.

The refusal to wear a diaper, now a necessity at night. "That's for children!" he protested. I tried humor, prancing around with the diaper on my head, pretending to be Queen Victoria. Finally, he was tucked in. Another day over without major mishap, another night ahead of us.

Our cat climbed onto the bed and stretched out on Bailey's stomach. Their noses almost touching, Bailey said to the cat, his tone triumphant, "Eva Truilly, Zora Diamond, Lulu Lawes!" These names were talismans: his boyhood schoolteachers. Prompted by the results of the nun study, Bailey had convinced himself that if he could remember their names, he would not succumb to Alzheimer's. I'd catch him at odd moments reciting this litany under his breath. "You know, I couldn't remember them this morning," he'd confided earlier. "They were gone. But just now they returned. They were sitting on top of my brain, fluffing their feathers."

The segment on the evening news spurred me to talk with Bailey about what was happening to him. I'd try this when I could, to see how aware he was. And I probably nursed the vain hope that he would become my partner again, rather than my charge, able to aid and comfort me as I him. Come back from wherever you're going, be adult and wise, understand how hard this is for me, too.

There was another reason: Bailey's mother had been an outspoken member of the Hemlock Society. And she'd carried out her belief, taking her life rather than enter a nursing home. Before Alzheimer's, Bailey often talked about her courage and his own commitment to "dignity in death." The catch-22 with Alzheimer's was that he needed to make his "exit" not in the extremity of the disease, but early, while he still had the ability to carry out his wish. While he still had some life left to enjoy.

Bailey's reaction was to turn to the wall. "Talk to me, Bailey," I said. "You always said you didn't want to live if you could no longer work. When you couldn't look after yourself." *Oh God.* I hope I was gentle.

"I *am* working. I *am* looking after myself." Muffled crying. "You will take care of it when the right time comes. You and the doctor."

"We can't, my darling."

"You will! You must!"

I tried to explain. But he wasn't listening. He had drifted back to Eva Truilly, Zora Diamond, and Lulu Lawes.

That night, Bailey woke again and again. The first time, he fell and became wedged between furniture. The second time, he stuffed his diaper down the toilet. The third time, having disposed of the diaper, he left a trail of urine on the floor. I slept through this last accident, to be shaken awake by Bailey. Stuttering badly, tears flowing in anguish, he pointed at the urine. I quieted him, cleaned up. Back in bed, he told me how disappointed he was with his life. This sense of failure was growing larger by the day. He carried it with him, shouldering it like a sack of coals.

9

Bart's secretary, who called her boss "Big Guy," complained about me to Hanny. Apparently I wasn't sufficiently deferential. I was puzzled; I didn't care enough to be impolite. Hanny decided to give me a lesson in corporate servility. Every phone call I made, I had to tell him what I planned to say. Every memo, e-mail, and buck slip I wrote, I had to pass by him. I obeyed his instructions to the letter, reporting all my communications, no matter how short or innocuous, down to the commas and periods. Finally, by the end of the week, even Hanny was tired of the charade. "Cath, give me a break," he said. "No, *you* give *me* a break," I replied.

That was also the week of the Elton John concert. Chuck had invited select members of his department to view Elton John at Madison Square Garden from

Niedecker's skybox. I tried to refuse but was told it was impolitic. We all dutifully assembled in the sky-box, stiff as store mannequins. Elton appeared, way below: a tiny, strobe-lit, herky-jerky clown manfully pounding the piano and producing a strained, indistinct sound. I looked around at my coworkers. They were jiggling their legs and mouthing along. They knew every word. Disdain bloomed in me like algae in a pond. If I didn't know that they were as adept at judging me as I was them, I would have felt sorry for them having me in their midst.

I never went out at night in those days. When I arrived home, despite yellow Post-it notes and phone calls reminding him of my whereabouts, Bailey was hysterical, red-faced, blubbering. He thought I had deserted him.

10

"Resist much, obey little," said Mike. Prompted by the words in the wrought-iron fencing, he was quoting Whitman. Mike was in a high mood. Bright sunshine and fitful wind signaled the end of another winter. Instead of huddling by doors or in recesses in the facade, smokers were spread across the plaza. We were on our bench. The river, the harbor, glinted. Oh Bailey, Bailey.

The cause of Mike's mood wasn't the sun but a fake memo that someone had written and placed in the racks where the analyst reports were displayed. The send-up had been provoked by a memo from the CEO. Ostensibly about the firm's strategy, it contained, buried deep in deathly prose courtesy of Chuck and Bart, the news of sizeable layoffs.

The fake memo had been photocopied and faxed so many times I had trouble making it out. Mike took it back and read the last paragraph out loud: "'In conclusion, we find ourselves at an inflection point. We must fish, cut bait, or get off the pot. These are difficult and exciting times, made all the more difficult and exciting by the lack of a coherent vision other than to sell the firm to the highest bidder. But difficult and exciting times require sacrifice. Making sacrifices is your job, not mine. As I always say, you are our greatest asset—our human capital. But you are also completely expendable. Onward, friends.'"

"Goodness me," I said, genuinely surprised. In my experience, admittedly short, the Niedecker rank and file did nothing but click its heels and salute.

Mike cackled, slapped his knees with the flats of his hands. "The security guys are running around trying to find out who wrote it." Niedecker, like other banks, employed a squad of retired policemen to frog-march wrongdoers off trading floors or out of offices. "You'd think they'd be happy to have a sign of life in the body politic. A pulse beats!"

"Who did write it?"

He shrugged and folded the memo into a precise

square. "Cone of silence, my dear. But it's not hard to figure out. Look for a banker who can write. And who is also witty. *That* limits the field." The wit in the memo seemed to me heavy-handed, but Niedecker was a buttoned-up workplace; those of us with funny bones panned for laughs like prospectors in a played-out gold field.

Mike and I had continued to meet on and off, and my knowledge of modern finance was slowly expanding. Balking like a nag in a steeplechase, I coaxed my mind to understand random walks, Brownian motion, game theory, fat tails, dynamic hedging, arbitrage in its many permutations. Mike's time was limited, but he enjoyed, as men do—if you will permit the generalization—instructing a woman.

And he'd opened up. In outward appearance, Mike was a Big White Man from Connecticut—Greenwich, to be exact—complete with wife, children, Volvo. But he was also a generalized radical, neither of the Right nor of the Left, but scattershot in his criticisms. Some might call him a fulminator. I fell into the habit of giving him a subject, usually one of the numerous financial scandals that occurred with regularity in those years—Joe Jett, Nick Leeson, Peter Young,

Orange County, Bankers Trust, Metalgesellschaft, Sumitomo, Daiwa—and he'd deliver a little lesson, a colorful sermonette. For the most part, I didn't mind his didacticism because I had hit the jackpot: access to the febrile, moody, bitchy underbelly of Wall Street. I primed and prompted and was rewarded with a flood of commentary.

Mike was schizophrenic in his attitude. He took a dim view of investment bankers, whom he characterized as digging clients' graves, helping them in, shoveling the dirt. ("Exhibit A: the Orange County bankruptcy. Traders sold that donkey of a treasurer, Robert Citron, dicey securities, and investment bankers launched public offerings to get him in even deeper. I rest my case.") An even dimmer view of the tendency to ignore the moral hazard involved in rescuing mismanaged financial institutions for the good of the entire system. ("Where's the incentive *not* to screw up?") A Leonard Cohen fan, Mike hummed "Everybody Knows" in the halls and elevators: *Everybody knows the fight was fixed/The poor stay poor, the rich get rich/That's how it goes, everybody knows.* I kid you not.

But Mike was addicted to the Street's energy, the

pace, the game. He was infatuated, too, with the idea of himself as a renegade, an independent mind. Or, more precisely, with the irony of someone with his views keeping an investment bank from running aground on shoals of sloppiness and stupidity, incaution and greed. While he claimed to be uninterested in bonuses and job security—the crude but effective carrot-and-stick of corporate life—he wasn't about to rock the boat or take his math skills anywhere else.

That day, he recounted a conversation he'd just had with Dan Napoli, head of Risk Management at Merrill Lynch. Napoli had told Mike that he always began meetings with head traders by asking, "What's worrying you?" "If those traders were honest," Mike said to me, "the answer should be, *everything*." He shook his big head. "Financial engineering—*perfumed* phrase. Derivatives—*freakish*." He made plugs on either side of his neck with his index fingers and lurched his upper body. Boris Karloff.

"'Behold the miserable wretch I have created!'" I contributed, remembering my Mary Shelley.

Mike gave no indication that he understood the reference, instead continuing with his train of thought.

"You know what the guys selling this bells-and-whistles stuff call it? 'YDWTK. *You Don't Want to Know.*' Muddier than the Mississippi."

"So Scholes and Merton are mad scientists?" Myron Scholes and Bob Merton were in line for a Nobel Prize for their work on a formula that had transformed derivatives from hothouse plants to unstoppable jungle vines.

"Smart guys. But their math works only in the short run." In full lecturing mode, Mike sketched an imaginary graph in the air. "The horizontal axis is time. The vertical axis is human involvement. Math only works right down here where the two meet. The more time that passes, the more human involvement, the more the math breaks down."

My mind took that hurdle, that water jump, with ease. As soon as humans entered the picture, any-thing could and did happen; all bets were off. "What about the hedging aspect? Isn't that the point of their engineering—to protect against the unexpected? Against outliers?" I was showing off the little bit of quant jargon I knew. Outliers are the phenomena that occur outside the normal distribution of events, in the so-called fat tails of probability curves. A thought scooted across my mind: Was Alzheimer's an outlier? Was I living my life in a fat tail?

Mike laughed. At me and at hedging. "The only perfect hedge is in a Japanese garden." This piece of humor wasn't original. "Look, Scholes and Merton are no different from the little guy with the big sunglasses and flashy belt buckle that catches the bus to Atlantic City or Saratoga Springs. He's betting on cards or horses. Scholes and Merton bet on swings and spreads, on volatility. The punter has a system. And so do they. That's all their formula is—a system to beat the odds. Not that they see it that way. They think they've beaten the odds, vanquished them. But these systems are never infallible. At some point, they *always* blow up."

"Taking risks is hardly new to Wall Street." I was beginning to bridle.

"The problem is size. They're not just muddier than the Mississippi—they could fill it. There are twenty-five trillion dollars of them out there—eighty trillion dollars by 2000, easy. *Bets*, not investments. *Gaming* contracts." Now he was hectoring me. Well, not just me but an invisible audience that no doubt included the SEC, the Fed, Robert Rubin, *everyone*. "Someone has to pay the piper. In the best of all possible worlds, everybody doing well, everybody flush with cash, no problem. But, to state the blindingly obvious, this is not the best of all possible worlds." More as an aside, he added, "Scholes and Merton are Panglossian. Incurably, irredeemably."

He ruminated for a bit—Mike was the only person I'd ever met who could truly be said to ruminate—and then said, "Which is a long way of saying there is no provision for illiquidity." Risk-management-speak for money tied up, coffers empty. "That river—in point of fact, it's a pyramid—will be the end of us. That, and global warming." His voice was regaining its normal, half-jesting tone.

"You exaggerate." I wanted to care but couldn't summon the energy. I wanted to be home, to be with Bailey, the nightmare to stop. And I wanted the voice—the indignant voice—next to me to shut up. To get angry at Scholes and Merton, at myopic quants, at derivatives, was as useless as getting angry at amyloid-beta protein. Things are always sundering, shifting, settling; this is the way of the world. It came to me that I was no longer even a vestigial radical, just a garden-variety fatalist.

"No. I'm not exaggerating. You know what they say?" He had fully recovered his droll detachment. "Only the *goyim* sell volatility. Jews are too smart to go near it." He flicked his cigarette stub into a planter. "Gotta go, kid." He was off at a fast amble.

11

Bailey's birthday. He loved jazz and had known many of the greats: Sidney Bechet, Jack Teagarden, J. C. Higginbotham, Miles, Coltrane, Gil Evans. I took him in a taxi to the basement of the HMV music store at Eighty-sixth Street. Buy anything you like, I said. He walked down the aisles of jazz CDs. These were my friends, he said, his voice soft and wondering.

Instead of listening to the CDs, he squirreled them away at the back of a closet. I puzzled over this, then realized that he could no longer operate the CD player. I tried to show him. He flew at me, grabbing me around the throat, pressing his fingers into my windpipe. I pushed him away. Thwarted, still possessed, he ran shrieking into the bedroom. Obscurely ashamed, I delayed for days reporting this incident to the doctor. An anti-psychotic medication was ordered up.

12

Hanny had somehow found his way to the Round-about Theatre for a performance of Strindberg's *The Father*.

"You must see it," he urged, leaning back in his chair, stroking his belly.

"I read a review. Sounds good." Mustering enthusiasm.

"It's about a woman who drives her husband insane." Sitting up straight now, elbows on his desk, massaging his hands. Insinuating. Sly.

"Really? How interesting."

Oh, for Pete's sake. I made my excuses to get out of his office. Buggerlugs had gone too far. There was only one thing for it: I had to develop my own "port-folio." A senior woman in the firm—one of two—had given me this advice. By "portfolio," she meant work that was clearly defined and could be defended when bonds fell out of bed or stocks nose-dived. When the blood flowed, as she put it.

I looked around for a corner of Niedecker I could colonize. The boys in my department were nothing if not assiduous in offering their services to anyone that mattered, with one notable exception: the head of Investment Banking, an Englishman named Horace. High risk for writers, they muttered, and steered a wide berth.

Horace was wreathed with gossip, like mist on a mountain. There was talk of an intern. That he'd had affairs with both men and women on his staff. That he was gay and the young women he squired were beards. This was retailed with moralistic glee by some; others indulged just to brighten their days. Horace, you see, had committed the corporate crime of remaining unmarried. For this breach, he was considered fair game.

The next time I saw Mike I asked about Horace.

"He's okay," Mike said.

"Why do Chuck and his boys tiptoe around him?"

"He doesn't suffer fools gladly. I once saw him turn

on Bart like an anaconda sizing up its dinner. Bart left the room *fast*."

I amused myself imagining Bart as a bulge in an anaconda. "They seem worried that he'll be the next CEO. It's a big topic of conversation."

"I bet they are. You'll like him. He's an oxymoron—a smart conservative." As was Mike's habit, he laughed at his own joke. "No, really. The last time I saw him he was carrying a volume of Trollope. But be prepared: He's a free-market fundamentalist. It's not ideological with him. It's *theological*." Mike deepened his voice, made the vowels plummy, and declaimed, "You cannot fight the markets! There will be blips. There will be pain. But the markets are virtuous!"

"Horace, I presume?"

"Yup. You gotta like the guy. He's probably never experienced pain—the economic kind—in his entire life."

I had nothing to lose. I volunteered to do some research for Horace, which went well, although I had no actual contact with him, only his secretaries. Then another project came up—a speech on the changing roles of banks in international capital flows—and I was summoned for an audience.

The route to Horace's office skirted the trading floor. I always paused on the balcony overlooking the vast, high gray space with its electronic tickertape snaking around the walls and terraced rows of traders and salespeople at their turrets, on the phone, drinking coffee, yelping, hollering, huddling. The floor was like the engine room of a battleship: thrumming with energy, giving off heat. Even the knowledge that what I was viewing was a bunch of fear-driven, foul-mouthed, sweating, no-neck alpha males in overdrive didn't make the floor any less seductive—the tangible heart of a place that dealt in intangibles. (There was a smattering of women, whom one could only admire, as one admires women Marines.)

Horace came from behind his desk to greet me. He shook my hand warmly, giving me the kind of conspiratorial grin that acknowledged what a farce this all was. Play-acting! He gestured to an armchair, folded his frame into another. He had spindly shanks and wore the kind of thin hose that requires garters. Graying hair clubbed back, emphasizing small, neat ears. Cleft chin. Unfolding himself to fetch something relevant to the discussion, he revealed a storklike walk. I later learned this was from a back injury—too much tennis and golf, too many airplanes. Every inch the deal-maker, the money man, the plutocrat, the princeling.

Most of the executives with whom I dealt bludgeoned you with their power. Horace didn't. He was like a fat man who eats two steaks at a sitting but does it with such delicacy that you don't notice, and later you wonder, how'd he get so fat? Horace charmed and flattered and amused, and before I knew it I was doing my utmost to charm and flatter and amuse back. With other executives, I felt like a tugboat guiding a listing liner into port. With Horace, there was, if not a partnership, an illusion of one. He was generous with his praise, his gratitude, the small gestures. Before I knew it, I wanted to walk on water for him.

We got down to tin-tacks: Margaret Thatcher and Ronald Reagan. "We owe everything to them," he said in his sonorous, brook-no-doubt, Oxbridge-accented voice. I demurred. Muttered something about bankrupt savings-and-loans societies and suffocating deficits.

A winning smile. An *indulgent* smile. The phone rang. He raised a finger, indicating that I should excuse him for a minute. I tried to guess his age, which I put at the other side of fifty, although it's hard to tell with people who are embalmed in authority, whose last spontaneous moment was in the cradle.

I glanced around his office. A grouping of Dorothea Rockburne paintings, mathematical in conception. A magnificent vanda orchid. On the coffee table, one of Trollope's Palliser novels, along with *Against the Gods: The Remarkable Story of Risk* and *Market Unbound:Unleashing Global Capitalism.* A couple of lucite tombstones, no family photographs.

"Why is it that you nearly always find the biggest brains, the *really* smart people, on the Left?" he asked, tangentially, when he hung up. I refrained from lobbing the question back: "Why do *you* think?"

"What's your background?" he continued. As if he —and Mother Niedecker—didn't know. When I finished my recitation, he said, "We need people like you at Niedecker. People who are different. Who will bring us fresh ideas." I hope I didn't simper.

My twenty minutes were up. In an instant, Horace switched off the warmth and camaraderie. He was beaming his light elsewhere, and I felt, for a moment, bereft.

Hanny was waiting when I arrived back in my

office, loaded for bear. The gist of his rant: Horace was not a leader. He did not have the character to be a leader. He was a lightweight. A Merchant-Ivory investment banker! If he became CEO, Hanny would have no option but to leave Niedecker. His fury was something to behold, his identification with Niedecker seamless. Horace's stock rose even higher in my estimation.

13

The disease was much worse. I had been told it would be like this, in abrupt shifts. No sooner had we adjusted to life reduced in yet one more way than the wheel was spun again, to have another skill disappear, more memories eclipsed, setting in motion a new round of adapting.

He wasn't sad or angry any longer. Eva Truilly, Zora Diamond, and Lulu Lawes had stopped appearing on the top of his mind, fluffing their feathers. His legs had become unstable, tipping him this way and that, and he blamed it on his shoes. Always his shoes. He refused to use a cane, instead propelling himself around the apartment by holding on to furniture and doorjambs.

He slept through the day, waking now and again to say he had work to do, although he was incapable of affixing a postage stamp, much less creating a collage. The journey to his desk began. Once there, he made a show of playing with his pencils and rulers, riffling his drawing pads. After a few minutes of aimlessness, he would declare he'd done enough, and the return journey to the bed began.

Friends visited, and he was cheerful, professing delight at seeing them, talking about future projects, important phone calls he'd received, a book in the works, a show at a gallery, filling in the gaps in his thoughts with orotund repetitions. Confabulating, as neurologists call it. He was careful not to leave his chair to show his infirmity. After they were gone, he invariably asked, "Who was that?"

To my consternation, some of these friends not only believed what he told them but could detect very little wrong with him. They called me to say that he seemed himself, a clear note of accusation in their voice, as if I were exaggerating his condition, making up the illness for some diabolical reason. I didn't bother to tell them that he had no clue who they were and forgot the visit within minutes of their departure. They probably wouldn't have believed me; I was learning that not many people can admit to being expunged from someone's memory, even by disease.

When alone with me, he mostly had on an expression of anxious vacancy. On good days, though, this was replaced by disbelief at his diminishment. That's what I remember: his startled, panicky disbelief. That, and how tired I was. I closed my eyes whenever I could. On the subway, in elevators, on escalators. I slept like a horse, standing up.

I had moved on from William Tabbert and Alfred Drake to Louis Armstrong: *When we are dancin'/ And you're dangerously near me/I get ideas, I get ideas . . .*

14

"Did you know," said Mike, "that Mussolini admired American corporations?"

I hadn't known. I had commented on the stifling, autocratic structure of corporations, ironic, at least for me, because I sprinkled speeches with references to a flat hierarchy and a collegiate, consensus-driven, meritocratic culture. Tra-la.

That morning, to illustrate the suppleness of our corporate hierarchy, Niedecker's CEO had turned to me and said, "Cath, you're only five removed from me." The CEO was a pedantic Midwesterner. As people say, to be polite, more a tactician than a visionary. Whenever I was in his company, I thought of Bill Murray taking the mickey out of his drill sergeant in the movie *Stripes* by telling him that he accepted his leadership because "Every foot needs a big toe." Our bland CEO was the quintessential Big Toe. "That's right," I replied, nodding brightly. In reality, a drop-off on the scale of the continental shelf existed between the CEO and me.

"Yeah, you're lower than whale shit," said Mike, when I relayed this to him. And then added the bit about Mussolini.

In front of us, water slapped against the hulls of fat fiberglass boats with names such as *Marjorie Morningstar, Powerplay, Excalibur, Momentum.* One of them had a miniature helipad complete with helicopter. Flags fluttered. Behind us, a bridal party with a photographer in tow traipsed across the pink marble paving. Asian and African-American couples treated the Winter Garden and the marina as if it were a giant photographic studio. It wasn't unusual to see three or four bridal parties waiting their turns at the most coveted spots: shy brides in frothy tulle veils, bridesmaids in low-cut satin, grooms barely of shaving age.

Derivatives-related scandals were piling up. Mike was keeping a running tally of the amounts involved: $12.2 billion.

"Where's the Fed in all this?" I asked, wanting scuttlebutt. I already knew he wasn't a fan of Alan

Greenspan. ("He's no god. He's just been lucky. Analyzes data but ignores human behavior. Says that's anecdotal.")

"Complicit. *Entirely* supportive of the notion that we should be a self-policing industry. Which is fine and dandy, except in good times, we get greedy. We get *lax*." He stopped, eyes unfocused, remembering something, then shook his skinny body as if to get rid of the thought. "Self-policing. Who are they kidding?"

"Why kill the goose? Where's the incentive in that? You'd think we'd cosset it, protect it in every way possible?"

"Well you might ask. Three words: Short-term gain."

"Two words, not three. Bankers are *that* stupid?"

"*That* stupid."

I had grown up thinking bankers were conspiratorial, controlled, far-seeing. If they were motivated by self-interest, they were also prudent. As one of many enlisted to help put out the five-alarm fires that regularly threatened to consume Niedecker, I was coming to the conclusion that the opposite was true. Bankers operated by the seat of their pants, crossed their fingers, winged it—anything but "proactive." They allowed markets and rogue traders to surprise them at every turn. They were as subject to fashion and flattery and incapable of objectivity or seeing the larger picture as ordinary mortals. As I'd quoted to Mike during one of our sessions, *Bankers are just like anybody else/Except richer*. Ogden Nash. Mike had snuffled his approval.

Mike turned the conversation to an item he'd seen in the *Times* about Iris Murdoch, who had developed Alzheimer's. He was a fan of her novels: "Philosophical. Not afraid of ideas." To my taste, Murdoch's writing was too ripe, too contrived. Anyway, all I read now was the financial press. I suppose Mike thought I would be interested. In his way, he was throwing me a bone of empathy.

"It's hard to imagine a mind like hers turning to Jell-O," he said.

"Yeah. Hard." Insensitive of him, but I didn't take offense. Instead, I was remembering a lecture given by Dame Iris at my university years ago: Murdoch and her husband, John Bayley, sturdy, plate-faced, English, dressed in matching duffle coats, and my boyfriend of the time and I—how old were we, seventeen?—also in matching duffle coats. Our lives in front of us.

"Engagé. That's what Murdoch was," mused Mike.

Engagé? I suppressed a snicker. Not a word you heard often in the hallways and cubicles at Niedecker. "Talking of engagement, why isn't anyone upset about the revelations in today's *Journal*?"

My fatalism had been shaken by a full-page article in the *Wall Street Journal* about a notorious racist who'd been a Niedecker client from the sixties up until a few years ago. Niedecker, which had funneled money for the client to a segregationist institute in the South, had defended itself with a specious argument, saying that the firm had taken the man on as a client in the sixties when attitudes about racism were different. "The clarity with which one sees issues today is different from thirty years ago," Bart had told the press. (I could picture him, a model of patient understanding. Bart always told us never to get angry at the press. Instead, we should pity them: their annual salaries wouldn't amount to a fraction of our bonuses.) Asked for complete records of transactions, Bart claimed they'd been destroyed in a fire. The dog ate the homework.

"Plenty of people were seeing racism with clarity in the sixties," I said to Mike.

"You're so naïve," he replied. "Bankers are pimps, enablers. They're"—he paused to find the exact word —"immoral. No, amoral. They hop on the money. What's in the caboose and where it's going, hey, who cares." He shrugged and turned his palms face-up in the classic New York gesture of disengagement.

Whose side *was* he on? "Tobacco companies are immoral. Children are amoral. Bankers are feckless." Sour.

"What on earth do you expect Niedecker to do?"

"How about starting with a full apology?"

"That would require bankers acknowledging a relationship between cause and effect. It would also leave the firm open to lawsuits."

We walked across the plaza to the Winter Garden, Mike with his hands in his pockets and whistling the tune of "Everybody Knows", which only succeeded in irritating me even further. I was tired of irony, of rue; we were cobwebbed with the stuff.

As a parting shot, I said, "We're pathetic, both of us." Mike just raised an eyebrow. He went back to his office to calculate how far Niedecker traders had gone out on a limb that day, and I to mine to finish a speech that Horace would give at Harvard to recruit MBAs to the firm and the free-market cause.

15

Bailey backed away from me, cowering in a corner of the bedroom. "I look after you! I cook! I sew! I iron! I polish your shoes!" He wept. He was crying because I was admitting him to a nursing home.

The call informing me of a vacant bed had come that morning at work as I was finishing my coffee and booting up the computer. I had been waiting on it for months, a packed suitcase at the ready in the back of a closet. The admissions officer gave me twenty-four hours to deliver Bailey or his bed would be taken. I stood at the window for a moment to summon courage, quell dread. From there I could see the Colgate clock on the Jersey side of the Hudson. The time dimly registered: 8.45. In front of it, a fireboat, testing its equipment, was spraying playful arcs of coruscating water high into the air.

What I was doing was against Bailey's wishes—or the wishes he had expressed when of whole mind. I could not help him end his life as he had asked; I felt it would scar my soul. Not that I believed in souls. I hope never to live through a day like that again. Even now, as I try to reconstruct it, I fall into a sinkhole of regret. I feel as lost, alone, guilty, as if it had just happened. If only I had found some way to keep him at home until he was completely oblivious of his surroundings. No doubt I did the best given the circumstances, but that's small consolation. I broke his heart. That damn disease.

The decision was made after consulting an assortment of professionals: a psychiatrist, a gerontologist, a social worker. They patiently pointed out that Bailey was as sick as his worst days, and the network of care I'd put together—a housekeeper, neighbors, students, hourly phone calls from me—was no longer sufficient. Nor could I afford or cope with round-the-clock homecare nursing.

I followed through with blinkered resolve: having him certified as needing nursing-home care; hiring an eldercare lawyer to place him on Medicaid; prepaying for his cremation as the law required; putting him on a waiting list at an institution near where we lived, run by nuns with scrubbed Irish faces and brisk demeanors. I tried to prepare him, repeatedly explaining the reasons, even gaining his approval. To no avail. His mind couldn't hold the information. When I arrived home and told him what was about to happen, it was news to him.

An old friend of Bailey's arrived to help. "Let's have a cup of tea," I said, and we coaxed him, whimpering, from his corner in the bedroom. Whimpering like Giulietta Masina in *La Strada*.

By the time we finished our tea, he had forgotten the home. "How about a drive?" I suggested.

We sat on either side of him in the cab, each holding a hand. He was merry. A child on an outing. But when we entered the lobby of the home and he set eyes on its infirm inhabitants, some clamorous and distraught, others inert and broken, he recoiled in horror. "No! No!" he cried, scalding us with emotion.

It was suggested I bring some of his favorite things to help him settle. I produced photographs, a bronze casting of a cat. He tore up the photographs and threw the cat across the room. He was beyond comfort.

When it was time for us to go, he turned on me. "You did this! You!"

We left him surrounded by rude misery and the stink of failing bodies. I had consigned him to a place where behavior was infantile, instincts animal. A place of last things.

16

The phone rang. Horace's name and extension appeared on the LED screen. I stiffened. Always pleased to hear from him; always put on notice not to twitter or be awed.

"Hello, Horace."

"Hello, Cath. What's this left-wing propaganda doing on my desk?" I had sent, via interoffice mail, an article by Felix Rohatyn from the *New York Review of Books*. Titled "World Capital: The Need and the Risks," it was hardly radical in my estimation, but everything is relative.

"I can't imagine who'd do that, Horace. What'll people say?"

"They'll say I'm broad-minded."

The speech had gone well. Horace was a demon about punctuation and English usage, gleeful when he caught me out in a mistake. In this he was no different from other banking executives: picky about small things, nonchalant about the big ones. The anxiety of their jobs had to surface somewhere. Missing commas elicited tantrums, but when big bets, big deals, were in the offing, they appeared carefree as Caribbean tourists.

Horace had ferocious powers of concentration. Compared to him, I ground my gears, juddered, stalled. But as to the lives most of us led, as to cause and effect, he was clueless. Boardrooms, airplanes, Town Cars, benefit dinners, boxes at the ballet, court-side at the Knicks and Wimbledon, the pavilion at Ascot—his domain was Olympian and circumscribed. I felt like an emissary from another planet.

I queried him on this one day after we had finished discussing a speech. "Horace, as an investment banker, your job is to look to the future, to advise clients on the wisdom of this merger, that acquisition. But it's been a long time since you rode the subway, went to a mall or a cineplex or a supermarket." If ever. "How do you know what's going on out there?" I pointed in the general direction of the world.

"I have analysts to tell me about trends." His lack of

curiosity staggered me. I remember that moment clearly. Horace had nicked himself shaving. A little piece of sticking plaster waggled above his upper lip. Swift's Cecilia.

"If you are never out and about, how do you know if the information the analysts are feeding you is correct?" The analysts I'd met were as capable of insight as goldfish. This last comment earned me a withering look and ended the conversation; I had gone too far.

All the same, Horace was curiously honest. Every Friday, rumors that Niedecker was about to be bought forced the stock price up. This was of interest to me because I wrote speeches claiming the opposite: Niedecker would never merge. The rumors were silly, we had the size to be a major player, bigness wasn't a virtue in itself, knowledge companies travel light. When I questioned Chuck about the truth of the rumors, he told me, smugness leavening his affability, that if anyone were to buy the company, it would be for our executive management, their intellectual capital. Of course, he added, executive management, mindful of Niedecker's proud history of independence and tradition of excellence, would never permit a merger. (Of course, behind the scenes, the firm *was* in constant negotiations with suitors.)

Horace flat-out contradicted Chuck's assumption about the value of our executive management. "There are thirty or so people in this firm who keep it going, who make the money. The rest is dross. That's what an acquirer would be after, that small group of people. And the firm's name. It's worth something."

"Are those thirty or so people executive management?"

Hearty laugh. "Goodness no! Executive management are *bureaucrats*."

Early in 1997, the Thai baht was devalued, and economies started to implode.

"Horace, should we worry?" We were hurrying from his office to the auditorium where the CEO was to comfort and succor "his" people, urge them on to ever-greater feats of teamwork. Despite his bad back, Horace walked fast, and I always found myself a pace or two behind him, struggling to keep up. Every inch the court retainer.

"It's just a blip. There will be pain, but the markets are efficient."

"Yeah. Right. But American investors, American

banks—the ones who caused the pain—are the least likely to feel it. Their losses will be covered." Moral hazard. I wanted to bring up the role of foreign exchange traders who had precipitated the crisis. The carrion birds of finance, they certainly weren't feeling any pain. But I already knew the answer: Mahathir Mohammed, prime minister of Malaysia, who'd railed against forex traders at an International Monetary Fund meeting, had been the butt of jokes on Niedecker's executive floor for days. The *gall* of the man. The *nerve*.

"Markets overshoot. They correct." Accompanied by one of his keep-to-what-you-know, don't-bother-your-little-head smiles.

Mike had nailed the accent and the attitude. But I had to give this to Horace: Mike and I, flotsam from the sixties, weren't the idealists, not by any stretch; he was. Horace idealized unfettered markets, which he genuinely believed had the power to create a brave new world. He also idealized Niedecker, which he saw as the last repository of honor on Wall Street. One got the impression from him that Wall Street in the past was made up of companies of knights errant bound by strict codes of behavior, saving not maidens but countries. In this regard, I could never tell if he was being disingenuous or naïve. Like any other Wall Street firm, Niedecker had its share of corner-cutters; money attracts them. But, again, everything is relative. If measured against some of its more relentless competitors, Niedecker could conceivably be called honorable.

"There will be pain." Please! By my lights, my leanings, Horace, insulated by wealth, cocooned in privilege, should be taken out and shot. But I enjoyed him, our conversations. Unlike my immediate managers, he wasn't a screamer, he wasn't poorly socialized, although I steered clear of discussions of race, feminism, homosexuals, the disabled; there were some rocks I didn't care to look under. He had intelligence and some wit. He had manners—he said thank you. He made my days easier. What can I say?

17

Bailey was a bolter. Even with his unsteady legs, he could find his way to the elevator and down to the lobby. He now wore an electronic monitor on his ankle.

"Where's he going?" I asked Evangeline, the Filipina nurse in charge of the floor.

"To find you."

For the first three months, when I arrived after work, he was always sitting on the edge of his bed waiting for me, his clothes in a neat bundle, his walking stick resting on top. I replaced his clothes on hangers, talking softly about my day, until he calmed down. He would tell me about all the work *he* had done, the phone calls, the new projects. He drifted in time and geography. I repressed the impulse to correct him and let him go wherever his mind took him. Bailey down the rabbit hole. His world had turned into one of his collages: swatches of memories, scraps of facts, found fears, discarded desires.

To get to Bailey's room, I had to pass a whiskered, pursy woman in a wheelchair. I always hurried by, averting my eyes. She passed the days knitting from a ball of twine the size of a cantaloupe and squawking like a macaw. "You bitch cunt niggers, get your dirty hands off me," she shrieked at the aides, none of whom was white. Accustomed to disinhibition—to use the clinical term—they ignored her. "Lace-curtain Irish," one told me, eyebrows raised a fraction.

Bailey refused to communicate with the staff, except to inform them that I was coming to get him, that this was all a mistake. Or, alternately, I had abandoned, divorced him. He began to panhandle, approaching visitors to ask them for money for food. I would find dollar bills squirreled away in his shoes or under his pillow and heartbreaking notes written in his deterio-rating hand: *Cath? My wife!!! Where are you? Please! Where are you?*

To my relief, he made a friend on the floor. Her name was Dolly, and she also had Alzheimer's. Her husband had preceded her at the home, in the same room, although nobody reminded Dolly of the fact. She favored peacock colors and black patent leather shoes and loved to dance. She talked to herself: an unceasing susurrus of complaint.

The friendship started because Bailey somehow discovered that Dolly had a pair of nail scissors and was willing to cut off his electronic monitor. He didn't know the monitor's purpose, just hated having a plastic gewgaw biting into his ankle. When I rounded the corner one day and caught them red-handed —she with the scissors, he with the hacked-off monitor—they turned their faces up at me, pretending innocence. What, *us*!

They began having meals together in the small dining room on their floor, Dolly giddy and Bailey adopting the pose of the long-suffering male. They both ate the same way, tiny portions, examining each mouthful and then chewing intently, as if they were discovering food. Around them, aides spoon-fed other residents, wiped chins.

Dolly invited Bailey to events in the home, singalongs and theme parties. I sometimes tagged along. The Hawaiian evening has stayed with me because the nuns wore hula skirts over their habits. The band, three men with shirts open to their waists, played Elvis Presley covers, and everyone in the room, helped along by stiff drinks—the nuns were not ones to deny their charges this pleasure—raucously crooned "Lawdy Miss Clawdy" and "It's Now or Never" along with them. In the middle of the last tune, Dolly dragged Bailey to his feet, begged him to dance, unaware that his legs weren't up to it. He stood in place, wobbly and dazed, while she waltzed around him, her movements elaborate, exaggerated.

Soon Bailey and Dolly were fixtures on the floor, sitting on chairs in the hallway, heads close together.

"What do they talk about?" I asked Evangeline.

"The home. The staff. Other residents."

I listened in whenever I could. In their minds, the home was a fancy hotel owned by a wealthy woman. Most of the guests did not belong there. Most of the staff, likewise.

"She has a big crush on Bailey," said Evangeline.

Dolly had indeed fallen in love with Bailey. "I don't care if he has a wife," she told anyone who would listen. "I love him. I will always love him."

Now, whenever she saw me, she scuttled away, blushing and angry. Bailey treated her importuning with grand indifference: a king getting his due.

Christmas at the nursing home was a big event. Decorations, trees, caroling, gifts, church services. I bought a scarf in brilliant blues for Bailey to give to Dolly. "Christmas? It's Christmas?" said Bailey. I called Dolly into Bailey's room and nudged him to hand over the present.

Dolly refused to take the scarf off. She wore it to bed. It became soiled, lost its flounce. No matter. She paraded down the hall, flinging it this way and that over her shoulder, as if she were a model.

Months passed, and she wouldn't part with the scarf, not even to have it washed. I bought her a new one, brilliant greens this time, but the ploy didn't work. The new scarf was stowed away in a bottom drawer.

The air in the home was hot and often foul. Despite the staff's best efforts, it smelled of full diapers and moldering laundry, creased flesh and overcooked food. On the way home, unable to clear the stench from my mouth and nose, I would stop between parked cars and retch into the gutter.

18

Horace wore his suits lightly; his colleagues came bubble-wrapped in their pinstripes. But on the day he had to give a speech to the firm's Women's Network, his tailoring was no help. He looked as uncomfortable, as unhappy, as a wet cat.

Fretting about the speech, he had enlisted me to come up with ideas. This was a problem. I kept my distance from diversity issues. I admired the people who put energy into the task, but they were Penelopes, always weaving, their work unraveling during the night. No matter how many speeches were given, targets announced, and initiatives launched, the numbers of African Americans, Hispanics, and Asians at the firm kept falling, with women making only the tiniest of gains. And, to be honest, I found young women bankers off-putting. They seemed to have perfected—indeed, made into an art form—the kind of hand gestures that showed off large diamond rings to maximum effect. And they could be more obnoxious, more condescending, than their male counterparts. While I marveled at their astonishing self-confidence, I also couldn't help but think, *For this my generation of feminists fought the good fight?* (The answer: *Yes.*)

Horace was of the opinion that minorities had the bank by the short hairs. (No, not his words.) I pointed out that Niedecker had yet to appoint a woman to its executive management team, par for the Street.

"They're in the pipeline," he replied. Ah, the fabled pipeline, invoked at moments like this. "And we have two women on our board." Miffed, defensive.

"Good for Niedecker! But two swallows do *not* a summer make." Trying hard to keep insolence out of my voice.

"You never miss a trick, do you?" And we turned back to his speech.

I warned Horace against repeating the CEO's mistake in front of the same group. Our Big Toe—so white, so male, so advantaged—had earnestly put himself forward as an example of diversity. If he, a

Midwesterner, plucked from architectural studies at Princeton, could succeed at Niedecker, anyone could, prompting head-ducking, teeth-gritting embarrassment. ("My favorite honky," commented one black woman to another, sotto voce.) I suggested instead to Horace that he empathize with the women by saying that being female in financial services was like playing tennis with the wind against you. One had to be careful using sports metaphors with career women, but I thought this might make the grade.

Horace forged into the meeting and spoke his piece. Polite applause. Then a panel of midlevel women took over. It became apparent that none of them thought that the wind was against them. Instead, to hear them tell it, they were making their way unaided except by their own talent and determination, vanquishing doubt by the excellence of their work. No mistake about it, these gals were fast-tracking to the top. For them, the pipeline was a greased waterslide at an amusement park. Bravado? All the same, standing there, at the back of the room, I felt like the Ancient Mariner.

19

Niedecker had two dining rooms. One was on the top floor, a soaring space with a maître d', attentive waitresses, exquisite art, and sweeping views of Ellis Island and the Statue of Liberty. Here executives and managing directors dined with one another or with clients. When so disposed, MDs invited subordinates to accompany them, in the name of mentoring. *De haut en bas* occasions, to be endured. The other dining area was a cafeteria in the sub-basement, where everyone below MD level amiably congregated to dissect the latest gossip. The food was awful, a notch above nursing home fare, but it was free.

I was lunching in the firm's cafeteria with Richard, the Human Resources officer who kept tabs on our department, when Mike walked by our table with one of his underlings in tow and nodded in my direction.

Although he was executive management, he sometimes came down here, as did the head of Emerging
Markets, which earned them points with the rest of us.
Rumor had it that Horace had once eaten in the cafeteria and pronounced the food excellent. It was also
rumored that he'd noticed someone picking through
the lettuce at the salad bar for the best bits and remarked that such behavior was a sign that Niedecker
was not what it used to be.

"Friend of yours?" asked Richard, an owlish fellow
who could be counted on to be amusing about
the antics of Chuck, Bart, and Hanny. A Niedecker
lifer, he had married his high-school sweetheart and
still lived in the same Long Island town where he
grew up.

"Not exactly. We meet outside on ciggie breaks. He
talks, I listen. He's got interesting views." I tracked
Mike as he went through the routine of pouncing on a
table before anyone else claimed it. He was unkempt,
stooped.

"Have you heard what he said at the last executive
meeting?"

"What?"

"Traders are maggots on the meat of capitalism."

I stopped hacking at the gray beef on my plate and poked instead at a clump of watery string beans. "Golly. Why'd he say that?"

"He was arguing against some proprietary trading strategy and getting nowhere. Lost it, I guess." Proprietary trading, the name given the in-house hedge fund activities of Wall Street banks, is a hot potato because, as with regular hedge funds, big money could be made—or thrown to the winds. Shareholders prefer steady fee-based earnings.

"What was the reaction?"

"Oh, I think they're used to it. These guys know each other pretty well. He's an odd duck, though. Good at his job, so they put up with his idiosyncrasies. Like Hanny."

Several weeks later, Chuck invited me to dine upstairs. As it happened, Mike again walked by, this time with the head of Private Banking, a tubby, disdainful Latin American. Jack Spratt and his wife. Mike nodded in Chuck's direction and then in mine.

"You know him?" asked Chuck. Casual. Ostensibly paying more attention to shaking out his napkin than his question.

I shrugged. "I interviewed him for a speech."

"Hmmm," he responded, imparting layers of corporate meaning with that one sound. "Bright guy. A quant's quant." He took a moment to enjoy his witticism. Chuck and Mike weren't buddies—Chuck was a Republican Party operative until he followed the money to Niedecker—but they had recently shared a fiftieth-birthday celebration on the executive floor; it had been my job to come up with jokes for the toasts.

"I hear he's been getting up noses."

Chuck grinned. "Yes. He has." Pause. "You've heard about that?"

"Just the bare outlines." As if anything of interest didn't make its way down through the ranks fleshed out, *replete*, with detail. Trickle-down gossip was much more efficient than trickle-down economics.

"Oh, he gets carried away sometimes. Probably going through a midlife crisis," said Chuck. Large smile, eyes periscoping the room. Chuck should know. He was divorcing his wife not for someone younger, blonder, and more adoring, as was usually the case, but for a sharp-tongued woman who'd had at least one facelift. Certain sections of the cafeteria had been humming like a high-tension wire with this news for months.

"How're things working out with Horace?" *Loaded* question.

"Fine."

"Cath, I know you are astute. But be careful. Complex character. Horace can't always, ah, be taken at his word." *Sheesh*. This was awkward. Like many people of charm, Horace was given to making promises. Anything to have you feel warmly about him at that moment. Promises that were not so much broken as allowed to slip from his mind as if they had never been made in the first place. But Chuck was that way inclined himself; his promises exited his mind backward, like tottering geishas.

"Uh-huh."

Chuck knew next to nothing about me, much less my capacity for astuteness, although he had been told I was "literary," which prompted his next remark. "You know, I've always wanted to write a novel about the financial world."

"Really!"

"A thriller. All the investment banks have CIA or State Department guys working for them. Filled with spooks! Being a banker is a good cover. The stories I've heard." True enthusiasm in his voice.

"Something along the lines of Michael Crichton? John Grisham?"

"Yes, that's it, exactly. I'm a big fan of those writers. Not that I get much time to read."

"Great idea!"

"Wouldn't mind having their bank accounts, either."

"Go for it!"

Chuck wagged his head, grinned goofily. I glanced across at Mike, engaged in intense conversation with his companion. In unison, they consulted their watches. Mike wore a plastic digital watch, the head of Private Banking something heavy and gold. A Jaeger-LeCoultre Reverso, if I wasn't mistaken. Showy.

I turned my attention back to Chuck. Observing him was as entertaining as watching Horace because he had an array of mannerisms, developed after he stopped smoking and drinking. Once, when he was having a conversation on speaker phone, I saw him whip out his comb and pull it through his hair, poke around in his ear with a pen, hitch up his pants, and then repeat the exercise, all the while laughing, doodling, gnawing on candy, consulting his computer. A marvel of multitasking.

Today, while he tore his bread into pieces and rearranged the cutlery and glassware, Chuck enlightened me on the latest advertising campaign. At that time, banks went in for big-picture, pious ads; they've since returned to selling products. The tagline for our new campaign: NIEDECKER BENECKE. BRIDGING THE GLOBE. BUILDING TOMORROW.

"That's a bit Clinton-ish," I said. Bridges were figuring large in White House speeches. This was before Monica, and the prudes of America began their year-long torture of the rest of us.

"He hasn't got a monopoly on the metaphor." His tone was warm, but it was a reprimand nevertheless; my opinion wasn't being solicited. Chuck was invariably good-humored, no matter his message, which is why he was liked. We were accustomed to the dissonance.

From then on, I limited my remarks to "Excellent!" as he outlined Niedecker's critical role in creating the infrastructure to ready the world for the twenty-first century. Providing financing for schools, hospitals, factories, dams, power plants, highways, railroads. Instrumental in making every nation competitive. I listened attentively, hoping to give the impression that

I was a good worker ant, masticating the information, turning it into wads of useful speech material.

After lunch, as he jabbed at the elevator button and bounced on his heels, Chuck asked, "Now, what were the take-aways from our discussion?" A consultant had given Chuck and his lieutenants some management pointers, among which was the advice to get us to repeat in our own words whatever it was they had said, in case we were inattentive, hearing selectively, or plain dense.

"Niedecker is serving humanity, sir. At its beck and call." We often added "sir" to our verbal communications with him, some of us spiking it with more irreverence than others.

"Please, Cath. Call me Chuck." Half-smiling, a little irreverent himself. Another jab at the elevator button. And another.

20

Bailey had a new room: fresh paint, crisp curtains, a view of the East River and Sotheby's. Prime New York real estate. But when I arrived after work, expecting to find him settled, he had disappeared. I searched. He was in his old room, curled in a fetal position on the bed, which had been stripped to its plastic mattress covering.

I placed geraniums on the windowsill of the new room, bought soaps and lotions, provided colorful patterned sheets, hung his collages on the wall, propped up photographs of his mother, of me. Out the window, I watched the limos and Town Cars arrive for auctions and entertained sour, uncharitable thoughts: *Spend your money, collect the finest. It's no insurance. You will all end up here, or somewhere like it. In ignominy.*

Within weeks of Bailey's moving to the new room,

his legs gave up altogether, making him dependent on a wheelchair. But whenever the chair was produced, he'd ask, "Who's that for?"

"You."

"Not me!"

"Your chariot awaits you, kind sir." Silliness still worked. He'd laugh and forget what had come before.

One day he pointed at his name on the door to his room and said, with great satisfaction, "An advertisement for me."

The next day, when we passed a linen trolley covered with a blue tarpaulin, he said, "A baby elephant lives in there."

"Really! That's interesting," I said.

Later, I told Evangeline about the baby elephant, expecting her to smile. Instead, she became thoughtful. "In the middle of the night," she said, "one of the ladies comes out into the hall and makes a ruckus. It sounds just like an elephant."

One of the stops on our perambulations was the home's chapel. Neither of us was Catholic—Bailey had been brought up a Quaker, and I, Church of England—but the chapel was quiet, and its stained-glass windows pretty. We'd sit near these windows, and I'd remember for him his childhood in New Orleans, our friends, our life together.

At Easter, Christmas, and important saints' days, to demonstrate my willingness to be part of the community, I took him to services in the chapel. The nuns would form a processional and walk down the aisle, giving their all to a hymn. Not a measured step among them. They tottered, lolloped, sloped. Some were round as toby jugs, others slight as sparrows. None could hold a tune. (Somehow I had thought that an ability to sing, because nuns did so much of it, was a requisite for taking the veil.) I loved them for it. And for their ready acceptance of Bailey and me.

Navigating the bureaucracy of the home required the same skills I was honing at Niedecker. The nuns were the administrators. In this role, tough cookies. Under them, in descending order, were doctors, nurses, aides, cleaners, with the ancillary staff—social workers, therapists, nutritionists—forming a caste of their own. An unbending hierarchy wasn't the only similarity to Niedecker. At meetings about Bailey's care, held every few months, the staff used the same language as my managers. They strategized, prioritized, everybody had to be on the same page. Heck,

I just wanted the aides to wash between Bailey's toes, monitor his bowel movements.

The nursing home was an Augean stable. Anyone with extra dollars hired a private aide if they wanted one-on-one attention for their "loved one." Now that he was in a wheelchair, I followed suit. He refused to cooperate with the first two I hired, glaring at them, sullen and refractory no matter what the inducement. Then I found Gwen. My age, Jamaican, she intuitively knew how to treat Bailey, according him boundless respect, swaddling him in affection. Her easy empathy matched Bailey's own. I often thought, watching Gwen, he should have married her and not me.

If it was sunny, Gwen took Bailey outside, to the East River or to an ice-cream store; if not, she found some activity in the home to distract him. If lunch was unappetizing, she wheeled him to a neighborhood coffee shop and fed him there. Gwen patronized Victoria's Secret, so they sometimes dawdled amid the store's lacy negligees and satin bras. She washed his clothes and linen, made sure he was always clean, his diaper fresh. "Girl, I'm here to give you peace of mind," she'd say.

I like to remember them having afternoon tea in his

room, eating chocolate chip cookies, watching Oprah, companionable as spinster sisters. Their TV viewing was often interrupted by the latest news on the Monica Lewinsky scandal, in full swing by this time. Gwen was an ardent fan of President Clinton, as were all the aides. He was *their* president. She didn't mind explaining to him for the umpteenth time what was happening. Bailey listened closely, pretending great interest but completely baffled. Then she shared with him her opinion that Clinton was being a man, no reason to get all heated up. Uncomprehending but vigorous agreement from Bailey. Expressions of disgust for Kenneth Starr and speculation as to what *he* did for kicks. Wide grin from Bailey.

Gwen had allergies. Her eyes reddened, she snuffled and sneezed. Seeing her like this caused Bailey to cry and fret. "She's sick," he would say to me, solemnly. "Is she going to get better?" We tried to tell him it was only allergies but couldn't dispel his anxiety. He broke his cookies down the middle, proffering half to Gwen. Ate only a little of his ice cream and then handed it to her. Spooned some of his lunch into the aluminum cover that kept it warm and wordlessly pushed it toward her.

Now, when I came to the home after work, instead of fussing with the one hundred and one things his care entailed, I could sit quietly with him, watching the news or reading to him, usually poetry. If he didn't understand, he enjoyed the sound of my voice. There always came the moment when I had to leave. I'd learned to lie or else risk anger or tears. "I'm just going out," I would say, "to get something to eat. I'll be back in a few minutes." When I returned the next day, he would clap his hands in pleasure. Sometimes, though, he would start crying, tugging at me, a five-year-old with his mother: "Where'd you go? This is *our* house. *Our* apartment. Where'd you go?" Or, his voice loaded with meaning, he'd asked, "When are we going to be husband and wife again?"

On the way home, I'd catch myself watching people hurrying along the street, preoccupied, places to go, missions to accomplish. Whatever their purpose, momentous or mundane, I envied them.

21

Looking over what I've written about Bailey in the nursing home, I realize I'm giving you the pathos of the situation, not the awfulness. A sanitized version: Alzheimer's sufferers say the darndest things. I want you to think of Bailey as sweet, as straining with all his being to keep his dignity, to stay true to his personality. Yet, as the illness advanced and his medications became less effective, there were days when he seemed to say, in effect, screw sweetness, screw dignity. Days when neither Gwen nor I nor anyone at the home could go near him. Days when he was barbarous, his room bedlam. Days when we shut the door and allowed him to remain filthy, unfed. Days when he spat, swore, snarled. Days when he smeared excrement on the wall, played with it. Days when he was black with paranoia, his mind coiled, suspecting even the vegetative residents of God knows what. Days when he inhabited a dim cave where the regrets, frustrations, and sadnesses from his life flew in skirling circles, clicking and squeaking, brushing their wings against him. Days when his face became sunken, hollow, his eyes feverish and haunted—a death's head.

22

"They can't do this. I won't be able to pay my rent. *Half* my income goes on rent. This is New York City, for chrissakes." I was in my office, on the phone, shouting at an eldercare lawyer. His name was Arnold Krooks, and he charged $400 an hour. When I hired him, I had found his surname amusing. Not any longer: I was in a bureaucratic vise. I could not afford a nursing home without Medicaid; not many can. On the other hand, to have Bailey placed on Medicaid, the law required that I, the "spouse in the community," be pauperized. (Unlike "strategize" or "incentivize," "pauperize" is a real word. And a real government policy: To impoverish.) I had no assets, no savings, only my income, and the Department of Health wanted half of it.

"You have to be patient and wait for a hearing."

"What are my chances?"

"I can't predict that."

"If they take half my income, I won't be able to afford pantyhose." Persiflage.

"They might take your age into account, the fact that you're still working. We just don't know. Most of the spouses in the community are in their seventies or eighties. They're not geared for someone like you." My office door was closed, but through the panel of glass next to it, I could see Hanny circling. He had the instincts of a vulture.

"So it's okay to pauperize a woman in her seventies? I knew the American healthcare system was fucked up, but *this* fucked up? Sorry. I swear when I'm upset."

"I noticed. Look, the Medicaid assessors used to have a heart. But people abused the law, passed all their assets to their children. So they're cracking down."

"Pauperize. It's more like pulverize." I glanced around my office. Piles of reports and presentations on every surface. The firm spewed these publications: countries and industries quantified and enumerated, predicted and forecasted, every which way. Bankers buried their heads in this stuff like proverbial ostriches or pulled it up over themselves like a down comforter, even though the methodologies and biases involved didn't bear thinking about. The material dated so fast that I requested a mini-dumpster every few months and threw it out. I kept only my dictionaries of famous quotations and joke compilations. They were perennial and indispensable, especially the golf quips.

"Out of curiosity, what will you do if you are unsuccessful at the hearing?"

"I'll leave my job. Then there won't be any income to halve. Or I could tip Bailey into the East River. No need for Medicaid then."

He ignored my sarcasm. "Would you do that? Leave your job?"

"Absolutely. What's the point? I only took it to see us through this." With the door closed, my office was stifling. Through some quirk, I only got air if the occupant of the office two down from mine left his door open. I glanced up at a piece of tape I had attached to a vent. I monitored it as a farmer watches the horizon for rain. Nothing. Not the tiniest flutter.

"Good. If that's what you'd really do. I'm asking because we're looking for a case to test the policy. You fit the bill."

Just what I wanted, to be a test case for the state's Medicaid laws. At one time, in another life, I would have come out fighting, but I didn't have the energy, and that, of course, was what Governor Pataki, Mayor Giuliani, and the Department of Health were counting on. The Job's wives among us don't have the time to brush their teeth, much less take on the government, and I was no different. I wanted only to make Bailey as comfortable as possible. I didn't want to crusade.

Hanny rapped on my door. I signaled for him to go away. "Arnold, if I lose, I'll have to fire Gwen." An image came to mind from the home the previous night: Gwen and I changing Bailey's diaper, Gwen on one side of him, me on the other, levering him out of bed and into a standing position, letting him support himself on the back of a chair, then briskly performing the task. Bailey stared straight ahead, firming his chin. After he was settled, Gwen asked me, not for the first time, if her hourly rate could be increased. Her goal in life was to raise the down payment on a city-subsidized apartment in the Bronx: "I want to make something of myself. Like *you*, girl." If it had been in my power, I would have given her the pot of gold *and* the rainbow. As it was, I felt as if I were being squeezed from every quarter.

"We'll cross that bridge when we come to it."

Hanny kept up his rapping. "I have to go."

"Try to put this out of your mind."

"I'll try." Fat chance.

I opened the door. "Everything all right?" asked Hanny, oozing solicitude, prospecting for weakness.

"Fine. Couldn't be better."

23

Mike and I were discussing Horace. *Everyone* was discussing Horace. He'd been elevated to president. Next stop: Big-Toe-dom. The firm convulsed, disgorged the also-rans, realigned. Chuck, Bart, and Hanny closeted themselves to read the tea leaves. They'd been happy to leave Horace to me, figuring I'd get chewed up and spat out, but all that now changed. They would throw themselves in his path, high risk or not. My outlook was dim; those boys could ace me in the same time it took to sneeze. As to Horace's opinion of them, I had no idea. When I ventured something mildly disparaging about Chuck to gauge his reaction, Horace remained silent, although he did raise an eyebrow a fraction at my indiscretion. Of Hanny, who could try the patience of a saint, he merely said, from time to time, *"Unhelpful* man."

"When Horace talks about honor, do you think he means it? *Really* means it?" I asked Mike.

"Sure he does. Honor among thieves."

Something *was* happening to Mike. He was almost always caustic, rebarbative, these days. He was becoming warty with bitterness. His nails were chewed ragged, his smoking hungry. The muscles in his jaw twitched. The lessons had stopped, as had his occasional polite inquiries about my well-being. No laughter high up in his nose.

At first I had supposed that worries about contagion from the South-East Asia crisis, now spread to South America, were putting pressure on him. Certainly I was hearing plenty about how derivatives were causing the contagion. "It's like having open drains running into the water supply," Mike said. Surprisingly, Horace concurred, although the language he used was less vivid. "Derivatives can magnify the effect of a shock in a geographic area or an asset class," he had me write in a speech, "and create unintended results where there isn't a true economic link." Here agreement between the two stopped. For Horace, the markets, not regulation, would quickly take care of those "unintended results."

But Chuck had guessed right when he said Mike was going through a midlife crisis. These were endemic among my friends. Some had found satisfying work that advanced their beliefs or at least didn't compromise them, but they were the exception. The rest were in disarray: consulting psychiatrists, knocking back antidepressants, going on traveling jags, changing careers, divorcing spouses, taking lovers. Among Niedecker executives, the most common symptom was the purchase of a vehicle capable of extremely high speeds, usually motorcycles: beetle-shiny BMWs and wasplike Ducatis that belonged not on the back roads of Westchester but in Formula One races, and ended up gathering dust in their garages. The manufacturers of these machines must have been delighted with this display of vanity. Even the Big Toe, not known for his imagination, now tooled around on weekends in a purple Porsche.

Mike's midlife crisis was taking a more bizarre form. The arrest of former radical Kathleen Power for her part in the 1970 shooting of a policeman during a Boston bank robbery triggered in him expressions of admiration for sixties terrorist groups like the Black Panthers, the Red Brigade, and the Baader-Meinhof gang. Reports of the dismantling of the Shining Path in Peru by Alberto Fujimori—another hero of Horace—elicited a similar reaction. "Whatever their methods, at least they weren't passive. They were *trying*," he said. "What am I doing? Helping ——" —he named the CEO— "get *Midas* rich. He could buy fifty purple Porsches if he wanted."

"Right. Long live the armed revolution," I muttered, not believing my ears. Many from the Left who lived through those times follow with interest and curiosity the fates of its outlaws and fugitives, the ones who crossed the line and embraced violence. I certainly do. There but for the grace of God go I, et cetera. But no one could rightly admire them. Understand them, put them in context, yes, but not admire.

Another time, he said, "With computers, you could bring the monetary system down. It would be easy. The whole frigging house of cards. You'd just have to lean on it a little. That's all it would take. Someone should. If a thick-headed know-nothing like Nick Leeson can bring down Barings, imagine what some-one with a *brain* could do."

"An imperfect system, but we haven't come up with anything better." Lame, I know.

"Yeah, yeah. Markets are not efficient, but they are the best method we have for determining price." Sing-song, quoting himself from one of our waterfront lessons. "That's beside the point. New York banks suck up money. They *hoover* it up. Determining price! Ha! That's way down the list of priorities."

I stood up to stretch, wondering whether I should make tracks. A quartet of bankers, sleek as tomcats, glided across the plaza. Foil-stamped in gray scarves, navy overcoats, black shoes. One said something amusing, the others laughed, exuding smug testosterone jocularity. Stereotypes. Something Bailey used to say to me when I was overly critical, too ready to sneer, surfaced in my mind: *Have compassion, Cath*. Yes. Right.

I looked down at Mike, hunched over his cigarette. To break his mood, I tried Ogden Nash: "'Consider the banker./He was once a financial anchor.'" No reaction. Another attempt. "I don't remember the rest of that piece of verse, except for this: 'The way some people sing whiskily,/Bankers are singing fiscally.' Terrible rhyme, no?" Not amused. "Look, if it bothers you so much, go and work for one of those watchdog groups that monitor the markets. Or a left-wing think-tank."

The financial world isn't a monolith of laissez-faire-ism any more than every Japanese was in favor of entering the Second World War; voices of wisdom and moderation exist, as they do anywhere else. They even exist in the executive suites of banks. Niedecker's chief economist was well known in the industry for his ideology-free reasoning. Another executive, a former World Bank officer, had no illusions about human nature. Whether they could win the day or be thought of as anything other than Cassandras was another matter. Even Horace, in unguarded moments, admitted the need for checks and balances, amelioration. He also admitted the paradox at the center of it all: To operate at their most efficient, free markets require transparency, but transparency requires regulation. Mike, though, was like a married man who falls in love with another woman and plots to kill his wife to gain his freedom, when the obvious solution is to drive off down the road to another life.

"There's no point. We're in a culture of deregulation. *Deep, deep* in a culture of deregulation. Supervisory standards are as weak as warm spit. Banks don't have enough reserves. It's a time bomb. Listen, I'm a risk manager. *I* know." Two thumbs jerking toward his chest. A fulminator gone rancid? Or a truth-teller?

While I thought his rants were a regression, I was not unsympathetic. Okay, a secret. In my wallet, I keep a scrap of disintegrating paper on which is written, "The revolution is magnificent, and everything else is bilge." Who said this and which revolution I'd forgotten, but I've transferred it from wallet to wallet for more than thirty years to remind myself of a time when I was young and silly, but cared. The idealism was magnificent, not the revolution.

Also, you have to understand that Mike and I worked in the modern-day equivalent of the court of Louis XVI. All around us, impossible sums of money were heaped on people who were no more deserving of it than any other kind of professional. Sure, they put in long hours in a Darwinian environment, but the same could be said of New York City public school teachers, who are paid a pittance and put harder to the test.

If stocks had stopped roaring upward, Mike would not have been as troubled, his commentary limited to humming Leonard Cohen. *Everybody talking to their pockets/Everybody wants a box of chocolates . . .* As it was, the longer the bull market trampled proportion in its path, the more Wall Street firms minted money, the angrier Mike became, the more he reached back to the slogans of his youth.

Strangely, for someone alert to irony, Mike never alluded to the fact that he was one of the people on whom gold rained. After nearly two decades of Wall Street bonuses, he could've opened a Porsche dealership himself.

24

A Sunday morning. With the assistance of a male aide, I loaded Bailey into his wheelchair, a model named Everest by its manufacturers.

"How about bagels at that nice café up the street? Best bagels in New York City," I said, bending to make sure his feet were squarely placed on the fold-down footrests. Excellent bagels *and* wheelchair accessible.

"We haven't got any money," Bailey said. Fretful.

"Don't worry. I have some." I patted my pocket.

"The keys. Have you got the keys to our apartment?" Querulous.

"Yes, I've got them right here." Patting my pocket again.

Bailey repeated his worries all the way to the café, and I kept reassuring him. Alzheimer's was surely sent

to teach me patience, not one of my virtues. I was getting good at it, though, not even feeling irritation, an
imperturbability that served me well with Niedecker's
vexatious executives.

I settled him at a table and went to stand on line.
Bailey always had a bagel with cream cheese and lox
and a bottle of Nantucket Nectars, a thick, sugary
juice drink. For me, fruit salad and black coffee.

Usually, we'd eat in silence. Perhaps I'd make the
occasional comment about the customers or the passing parade of joggers in Lycra or sweats, fathers
having quality time with small children, single women
with streaked hair and small dogs. That day, though,
I needed to talk. "Mike once told me that Mussolini
admired American corporations," I began. Utter
puzzlement on Bailey's face. I backed up. "I've mentioned Mike to you before." A moue of jealousy. "Just
someone I work with, sweetie. Do you remember
where I work?" He stuttered an incoherent answer.
"Down on Wall Street. Writing speeches. What Mike
said about Mussolini made me realize something.
Hardly an original thought, I'm sure. The United
States is a democracy, and yet it's powered by autocratic corporations. Its engines are fascist. Nothing

democratic about them. Paradoxical, wouldn't you say?"

Bailey was having trouble with his bagel. Warming to my subject, I kept on talking while cutting the bagel into smaller pieces, wiping a dob of cream cheese from his collar, giving him a fresh napkin. "There's a pretense at democracy. Blather about consensus and empowering employees with opinion surveys and minority networks. But it's a sop. Bogus as costume jewelry. The decisions have already been made. Everything's hush-hush, on a need-to-know-only basis. Compartmentalized. Paper shredders, e-mail monitoring, taping phone conversations, dossiers. Misinformation, disinformation. Rewriting history. The apparatus of fascism. It's the kind of environment that can *only* foster extreme caution. *Only* breed base behavior. You know, if I had one word to describe corporate life, it would be 'craven.' *Unhappy* word."

Bailey's attention was elsewhere, on a terrier tied to a parking meter, a cheeky fellow with a grizzled coat. Dogs mesmerized Bailey. He sized them up the way they sized each other up. I plowed on. "Corporations are like fortressed city-states. Or occupied territories.

Remember *The Sorrow and the Pity*? Nazi-occupied
France, the Vichy government. Remember the way
people rationalized their behavior, cheering Pétain at
the beginning and then cheering de Gaulle at the
end? In corporations, there are out-and-out collabor-
ators. Opportunists. Born that way. But most of the
employees are like the French in the forties. Fearful.
Attentiste. Waiting to see what happens. Hunkering
down. Turning a blind eye."

Bailey was now sucking noisily on his straw. People
glanced in our direction. "The bottle's empty, sweetie.
Would you like another?" A wordless no. "You know
what cracked me up in *The Sorrow and the Pity*?
Never forgotten it. How the society ladies in Paris
raised money to plant rose bushes along the Maginot
Line so that the soldiers would have something
pretty to look at. What were they thinking? Rose
bushes!" I speared a chunk of cantaloupe. "American
corporations. Invented to provide goods and services,
but that's the least of it now. Which brings me to
globalization. Better not get me started."

Bailey wasn't about to get me started. Instead, he
was examining his plate for morsels. Nothing wrong
with his appetite. Should I get him another bagel?

No—the line had grown. I stayed where I was. "I know. I'm simplifying. Sure, some corporations are restrained in ambition, truthful. Not all boards have directors who are pompous old boys. And Philip Larkin's toad squats in all of us. People are people, inside corporations or outside." Bailey squirmed in his seat. Diaper probably needed changing. "Sorry, darling. Got a bee in my bonnet today. Shall we go?"

25

"Hedge funds eat like chickens, shit like elephants."
Mike, of course.

"Shit money or trouble?"

"Trouble." He stamped his feet. "Fuck, it's cold."
We were huddled in an alcove near the revolving
doors of the Winter Garden, smoking with our gloves
on, talking in monotones, the frigid air not allowing for
emphasis. The plaza was littered with lumps of dirty
ice-hard snow. I was nearly six years into the job. Six
years into the disease.

Hedge funds were Mike's latest target for demo-
nization. The term "hedge fund," I was learning, is a
misnomer, implying as it does the safety net of hedging one's bets. Instead, they are a financial no-man's-
land, completely unregulated, where the "aggressive"
money goes to multiply itself. Unregulated because

the investors—once wealthy individuals but now increasingly foundations and pension funds—are assumed to be big kids and able to take care of themselves. Hedge-fund managers get a piece of the action as well as a fee, which encourages fiscal daredevilry. At last count, $400 billion was in hedge funds, an unprecedented amount. It's midnight. Do you know where your retirement money is?

Mike would rattle on about martingale theorems, how models for convergency trading de-emphasized the past, how Schumpeter said risk was not a source of profit, how a lot of hedge-fund speculation was not only opportunistic but antisocial, dependent on bad things happening somewhere or forcing them to happen. To hear him tell it, hedge funds had tails, horns, cloven feet, pitchforks.

Most of what he said I found a slog, but martingales managed to snag my attention because of the etymology. In the part of my brain reserved for trivia, I'd stored the knowledge that a martingale is a forked strap that stops a horse's head from rearing. Never having played cards or gambled, I didn't know that it was also a gaming strategy, although the two meanings are connected, if one thinks of the strategy as a method for harnessing luck. It's when a stake is doubled until the cards or the numbers turn favorable. You can clean up—if your money holds. Martingales are banned in casinos because of the ease with which gamblers can get clobbered, but not in finance.

In essence, at least according to Mike, this was the strategy of one hedge fund in particular; its traders bet on spreads converging and stuck with the bets, borrowing vast sums to keep them in business until they won. A daddy of a double-or-nothing urge. You will have heard of the fund because it became the financial world's Icarus. The fund's partners were notoriously secretive, even for hedge funds, which are accountable to no-one. After its wings melted, debate raged about who outside the fund knew the extent of its borrowing, the nature of its ill-judged bets.

Mike knew, as I found out that day. An old Harvard friend who worked at the fund had let slip the degree to which the fund was in the hole and some of the positions they were taking. "Lunacy," said Mike. "They're leveraged thirty to one. They have around $4 billion in assets, which means they've borrowed $120 billion. That's not nosebleed leverage. It's hari-kari leverage." Leverage: perfumed word for "debt."

"That's not counting derivatives. Their derivatives book is around $1.25 trillion. You know what their ambition is? To have zero capital and infinite leverage. Wouldn't we all! Pah!"

"So? Who cares if the rich fall on their faces? Lose a billion or two?"

"This is too big. *Way* too big. Sure, if things stay in their favor, they'll keep making gazillions. If they don't—one of those fat-tail events—they'll go bank-rupt quicker than a snake disappears down a hole. But with those sums, so will anyone who's invested in them, anyone who's taken the other side of their trades. That means most of the banks on Wall Street."

" You'll tell ——, of course." I named the CEO.

He didn't hesitate. "No. I won't. I want to see what happens."

I was dumbfounded. Catching my expression, Mike said, "At heart, you're a goody-two-shoes, aren't you? He wouldn't listen to me, anyway. Risk managers are for show, you know. I've told you before"—he ges-tured toward the deserted bench and empty marina— "VAR and Raroc are full of holes. More flaws than our president." As much as the cold allowed, he smiled. VAR—Value at Risk—and Raroc—Risk-Adjusted

Return on Capital—were the financial models on
which Wall Street was dependent for calculating
possible losses. "We're window dressing, just like the
speeches you write. We keep shareholders and banking analysts happy. We're Snoopy blankets."

He paused. Mike had gone over the edge. Flipped.
He returned to the subject of the CEO. "Listen, Cath,
I can't believe he doesn't know. If I know, he knows.
But I gotta tell you, he thinks these guys can walk
on water. They *all* think that." Expansive gesture to
include all of Wall Street.

Flipped. Should I bring this up with Horace?
Hardly my place. Flustered, I changed the subject.
"We should go work for Philip Morris. I bet they allow
their employees to smoke inside."

"You'd work for one of the merchants of death?"
Mike was momentarily sidetracked.

"Yeah, why not." I didn't mean it. I was just practic-
ing repudiating the last of my principles. "We're only
at one remove from companies like that. We provide
the financing for all sorts of dubious enterprises."

While Mike lit up a second cigarette, I tried another
conversational gambit. "Sad about our free lunches."
In the name of cost-cutting, the Big Toe had done

away with our free lunches, in-house medical services, and flowers in the lobby. "That's made the natives restless. Some are saying it's the beginning of the end. We'll be sold before the year is out."

Mike ignored me and started up about how there should be limits to the amount of credit extended to hedge funds. My mood turned cranky. Oh, go and volunteer at a nursing home, get some perspective, I felt like telling him. It occurred to me that Mike's ever-increasing, ever-more-shrill prognostications of doom were a martingale of sorts: One day he'd hit payola. If he didn't get fired first.

26

At the first opportunity, I told Horace what Mike had said about the hedge fund. Call me a corporate suck-up, an imperialist running dog. Call me craven.

At Mike's expense, I was trying to impress Horace, demonstrate that I was "in the loop," understood the subtleties. Speechwriters have an anomalous place in corporate hierarchies, near the center of power and yet of no real account. Also, for all my railing about city-states and occupied territories, I'd come not just to like Horace but to trust him, in a fashion. I worked with him every day; familiarity wasn't breeding contempt. And not only him. In one part of my mind, I couldn't believe that these men were operating entirely out of self-interest. I would never have admitted it, but I had begun to buy into the propaganda I wrote. It had crossed my blood/brain barrier. Maybe

Hanny was right: *You'll become conservative working here. You wait and see. Everyone does.*

I'm underplaying this about-face, I know. Embarrassed, of course, by the sniveling ease with which I betrayed Mike in order to ingratiate myself with Horace. I could rationalize it by saying you had to be there, caught up in Horace's force field, to understand. But that would be truly spineless, truly disingenuous. As it is, there is no shortage of disingenuity on Wall Street. Thick on the ground as mud on a farm in winter. I won't add to it.

Horace showed no surprise. He picked up a fountain pen from the vast collection arrayed on his desk, took off the cap, examined its nib. He gazed at the orchid that was currently gracing his office. He checked his watch—a Swatch. He had a thing about Swatches. "I'll look into it," he said, "but I have every faith in —— and ——," naming two of the principals of the hedge fund. "We go back a long way." Horace was loyal to his friends, more loyal at times than he was smart. *Bankers are just like anybody else/Except richer.*

27

Niedecker's managing directors, many of them ordered back from vacation, filed into the auditorium. When all the seats were taken, they lined the walls, crowded the doorways. Russia had done the unthinkable: devalued, defaulted, refused to honor its coin. Not even the sleaziest Latin American dictatorship had stooped to that. To make matters worse, the IMF had balked at pumping more money into Russia; their last loan had landed in Swiss and Channel Island bank accounts without passing Go. Investment banks and hedge funds, up to their necks in derivative contracts involving Russia, had to pay the piper.

Mike was as happy as a pig in mud. This was the mayhem he had predicted. He had phoned me the day before, hooting in his glee. "Finally, *finally*, the IMF did the right thing. Took away the safety net. Invoked moral hazard. Maybe the banks will begin to think twice about where they dump their money. Lift up the carpet and see what's under those *innovative* derivatives contracts." In our brochures and speeches, we never used the word "derivatives" without qualifying it with "innovative," hence the sarcasm.

"How's your hedge fund doing?"

"*Major* trouble. They're being disemboweled, dismembered. Their money is running out." He paused to catch his breath. "Fiscal hygiene at last. It's gonna be interesting to see what gets flushed out. *Who* gets flushed out. Because it won't stop with them."

"As you told me. Have you sounded the alarm?"

"For you to guess, me to know."

"Good luck. Just remember, the dice are loaded. Everybody knows." A reference to his Leonard Cohen song.

"Not this time."

And then an emergency meeting to rally the troops. Horace was in the front row, along with other members of executive management, pictures of gravity, dispensing with their usual minuet of affability. I could make out the back of Mike's head in the second row. Chuck, Bart, and Hanny sat in the middle of the

KATE JENNINGS

auditorium, Chuck smiling, Bart scowling, and Hanny swelling like a puffer fish at being included in an important occasion. I stayed out of everyone's way at the back in case my presence was questioned.

The CEO took the stage: "Recent global market turmoil has tested Niedecker people in unprecedented ways, under conditions never before experienced. What Russia did was much worse than even the most bearish prediction envisaged. What happened was inconceivable. It broke all the rules."

Normally, the CEO's face was as inexpressive as, well, a big toe. This day, though, he looked—there is no other word for it—gob-smacked. And his burly body, the kind that occupied every inch of space available to it, sagged.

He offered up pap about the firm's ability to add value for clients in turbulent times. He asked "his team" to keep a long-term perspective. He used "impact" as a verb seven times. The words "robust" and "opportunity" were noticeably absent from his vocabulary. The bankers, usually expert at hiding nerves, responded in a variety of ways: fiddling with the fat knots of their Hermès ties, putting two fingers between the collars of their shirts and their necks to allow the blood to flow, checking creases in trousers, twisting wedding bands, smoothing hair. One even pinged his braces. Busier than kindergarteners. Yearly reviews were on the horizon, along with "envelope day," when they learned the size of their bonuses.

Horace's turn to speak. He began with a joke of sorts: "We financiers like to think we are in control. The events of the last week have shown us how untrue that is." Subdued laughter. He talked about financial models failing despite far-seeing stress testing. He reminded us that no one is master of the markets, no one can outwit them. He alluded to the IMF money now in secret bank accounts. His message: Faulty models, headstrong markets, the Russian oligarchs— they were at the root of Niedecker's woes. As if bankers were innocent bystanders and not the markets' puppeteers; as if they had not constructed the models with the express intention of taming the markets, harnessing them, stopping the head from rearing; as if they had not joined the scramble to take advantage of Russia for fear of being left out of a killing. As if elves at the bottom of the garden were responsible. Shame on Horace. He sounded for all the world like an alcoholic who blames the bottle and not himself.

Questions from the floor. Niedecker corporate events were scripted down to a fare-thee-well, as stylized as a Noh drama. The questions were scripted, too, by Hanny, planted by Chuck and Bart. This day, things did not go as planned. A banker standing to the side flagged the CEO and asked a genuine question, an event as unthinkable as Russia's default: "Why was so much of our capital invested in a country that has never had a market economy, never had the civil institutions that make a market economy possible? Not only that, a country run by gangsters. This is not a secret. Anyone who reads the *New York Times* knows it." He had a slight Southern drawl.

The assembly squirmed as one. The CEO, his stolid demeanor and square shoulders resurrected by this impertinence, took his time in answering: "First, we had no reason to believe that Russia wasn't attempting serious reform. All the indicators suggested this, as did our field research." A double negative, to be avoided at all costs in the corporate world, where the spin is to accentuate, relentlessly, the positive. *Always* use the active voice, *never* qualify. As for the field research, even I was aware that Niedecker's research team in Russia consisted of a mid-level government employee who ducked out from her job to report from a hotel-lobby phone. "Second," he continued, "it's a risky world. Always has been, always will be. That's how we make money, how we sometimes lose it."

The banker who asked the question was *dead*. Knowing that, he persisted. "With all due respect"— involuntary titters, choking coughs—"for a long time now, the word on Russia, the joke about Russia, has been that it was a submerging market, not an emerging one. How is it that we were so exposed?"

They did know about Russia, some of them, sort of. Financial services companies aren't seamless, their PR notwithstanding. They are an agglomeration of fiefdoms. The left hand doesn't always know what the right hand knows. Another way of looking at it, courtesy of Mike: The information available to firms like Niedecker is shallow but wide. What traders know is deep but narrow. A recipe for trouble.

The CEO hunched over the lectern and grasped it with both hands as if he were a quarterback and the season depended on him. "After the last infusion of money from the IMF, we saw trouble on the horizon and cut our positions aggressively. And we'll keep doing that. This is not easy because these positions are very knotty, very complex"—*you have to understand the subtleties*—"but we will be successful. We *thrive* in times of challenge." He finished with a non sequitur, of which he was fond. "We are an organization with a global culture and a global value system." He strode offstage, heading for the safety and silence of the executive floor.

The bankers filed out, no more reassured than when they went in. Surely, in their heart of hearts, they had to admit to the real nature of the global financial markets: perilous, jerry-built, mortared with spit and cupidity, a coat of self-serving verbiage slapped on to tart up the surface and hide the cracks.

28

Bailey was hemorrhaging. The night nurse stuttered this news into the phone, apparently unnerved by the amount of blood. I pulled on clothes and arrived at the home just as they were bringing Bailey out to an ambulance. He was glassy-eyed, clammy, swooning; the medics were jovial. It was two in the morning, crisp and cold. His time to die.

The ER at St. —— is disorderly, crowded, ungentle; any New Yorker will tell you that. Walls, ceilings, floor tiles—they are impregnated with fear.

"He's in the final stages of Alzheimer's," I told the triage team. "He's DNR. Make him comfortable, please, but nothing else." The words came out clumsily. I was surprised to hear them. Let this person, who is dearest to me, who is my family, die.

They paid me no heed. I might as well have been

invisible. They consulted his medical records, which had come with him from the home. A plump bag of blood appeared and was attached to an I.V. pole.

"What are you doing? Why are you transfusing him?"

They were deaf. I asked for the doctor in charge. He had a damp, limp handshake. He didn't bother to hide his impatience.

"I beg of you, return him to the nursing home."

"He will die," said the doctor, "if we do that."

I changed my tack. "Palliative care. Don't you have palliative care?"

"No need for that." Stern.

"We have living wills. Healthcare proxies. No extreme measures."

The doctor turned away, flicking me from his consciousness as if I were lint.

Bailey kept on hemorrhaging. The transfusions continued apace. His skin became translucent: cold, colder, coldest. Around seven in the morning, he stirred. He opened his eyes and smiled shyly. "Cath," he said, "the party's over."

I searched his face, shocked by his lucidity. Did he know what was happening? A few minutes passed in silence, and then he gestured at the other patients on gurneys—firemen suffering from smoke inhalation, an electrocuted electrician, a construction worker with a crushed leg, a couple of asthmatics—and said, with utmost seriousness, "Do *all* these people have invitations?"

Bailey was admitted to a ward in the hospital. Interns gathered around his bed, white-coated ghouls strung with stethoscopes. "What year is it?" "Who is the president?" Solicitous at first, then, when he didn't respond, loud.

"He's not deaf. He has Alzheimer's." Fluttering at the edge of the group.

"Who are you? His daughter?"

"His wife."

Raised eyebrows. The interrogation continued. "Where are you?"

"In a hotel on Madison Avenue," said Bailey.

"No! You're in a *hospital*." Loud *and* impatient.

Bailey pulled back into his pillow, terrified.

"He needs his medication," I told them, "or you won't be able to control him."

"The elderly are overmedicated." Accusing.

Within an hour, Bailey had pulled out all his tubes and drips, spraying the room with blood. The nurses berated him, cleaned up, reinserted everything, only to have him pull them out again. He heaved himself out of the bed and fell to the floor, where he lay, beached. They strapped him to the bed.

The next morning, to prevent bed sores, he was removed from his bed and placed in a restraining device called a Johnny chair. Gwen, who came when she could, was sitting with him. I greeted him in my usual way, my cheek against his concave, stubbly one. No answer. He didn't recognize me. From time to time, he had forgotten my name but never who I was: his protector. Gwen looked stricken for me.

That day, all he wanted was to get free of the chair. The angle of it, the confinement, hurt him. He banged and pushed at the chair's railing, snorting with frustration. When that didn't work, he began to examine its construction with fierce absorption, to no avail.

The care in the hospital was minimal and grudging. It became even less so when the hospital aides learned I had Gwen. I arrived one morning to find his bed a swamp, his body smeared with excrement. Beyond rage, only wanting him clean, I went to find a nurse. They sat with the interns at computer terminals, tap-tapping. Irrationally, I felt what was happening was my fault. I found a basin and towels. Gwen arrived and together we cleaned him. He was oblivious to our ministrations. An animal determination to survive gleamed in the back of his lusterless eyes. Pinpricks of life surrounded by dullness.

Tests were conducted and botched. The cause of the hemorrhaging was never found, and Bailey was returned to the nursing home, where flu was raging. He caught it, developed a lung infection, and, for the second time in a month, hung on the edge of life. He was dosed with quantities of antibiotics, again without my permission, and recovered. Pneumonia used to be called the old people's friend. Not any longer.

It was customary at the home to line up residents far gone in their diseases near the nursing station, where they could be watched with the least trouble. They sat strapped into wheelchairs, lolling, slumped, empty-eyed, indifferent to their surroundings, some silent, some gibbering, occupying a slope of hell. Bailey joined the line for the first time, sitting upright and stiff, but as vacant as the rest. His last wits had been shocked out of him. He had forgotten to remember. Finally, reduced to a nub. Seeing him in the line, I gave up.

29

Reconstructing those last months, I suspect—I know!—I was not in my right mind. All the same, my mind—my wrong mind?—was made up. Scar on my soul be damned. He'd asked me to take care of it when the time came. Now I would. Mrs. Death. Not an assisted suicide, though. A mercy killing. Merciful for him. And merciful for me. I was on a life raft, Bailey was in the water, going down but holding my hand with an iron grip, pulling me after him.

I arranged that in the event of another emergency he be taken to a hospital that might be more respect-ful of our wishes. Then I obtained the pills for an over-dose from a doctor who was part of a guerrilla network willing to help in these situations; many have trodden the same path. To reveal more would be to incriminate others. Accessories to manslaughter, if not murder, according to the laws of New York State.

I *can* tell you that the doctor's office was one of those thousands of windowless shoeboxes that the medical profession inhabit on the ground floors of apartment buildings on the Upper East Side. Pin-tidy. An arrangement of silk flowers. A huge computer, which she consulted occasionally. She'd done her homework on Bailey, on me.

After we ran through Bailey's medical history and recent experiences, we discussed ethics. I'd read Peter Singer, Ronald Dworkin, and Sherwin Nuland early in Bailey's illness, consulted books with titles like *The Moral Challenge of Alzheimer Disease*. I knew about slippery slopes and the argument that what healthy people want in the last stages of life might not be the same when they get there. That is, if Bailey had a mind, he might tell me he had changed it.

She asked me if I had fully considered the risk I was running. Truth be known, I was past questions of risk or morality, boxed in, as animal in my instincts as Bailey. All I knew was that living wills and healthcare proxies could be blithely ignored, that common sense concerning the final stages of disease is often absent.

All I knew was that it was time. Stand in judgment if you like. If you must.

The doctor handed over the pills in a small turquoise box. A Tiffany box. Put her arm around my shoulder as she walked me to the door that let out into the street.

30

The hedge fund was duly disemboweled, dismembered, and Mike's tally of derivatives-related scandals leapt into the stratosphere. "All the king's horses and all the king's men aren't going to put that hedge fund together again," he joked. He was wrong. The banks resurrected the fund. The excuse given was that its bankruptcy would imperil the entire financial system. What they meant is that it would imperil them; *their* losses would be "unsustainable." In the best tradition of Wall Street, they were saving their own bacon. The heck with moral hazard.

The events surrounding the rescue are well documented. My view of the shenanigans was limited to glimpsing Horace throwing on his jacket as he ran through the Niedecker lobby on his way to the New York Fed building, where the bail-out negotiations were held. He was not so much running as scuttling. Horace, scuttling! This *is* major, I can remember thinking. These guys *never* run, unless for a plane. As the drama unfolded and the rationalizing and the spinning of facts began in earnest, my incipient conservatism collapsed. I was back where I began, only more so, cynical as an old-time, hard-bitten, newsroom journalist. And as outraged as if I'd been sold the Brooklyn Bridge.

When it was over, someone had to take the bullet. Another Wall Street tradition. At Niedecker it was Mike. He wasn't even allowed to clean out his desk. Over at Merrill, Dan Napoli took extended leave. Other risk managers and a slew of traders were given their marching orders or quietly disappeared from the scene. A couple of senior executives had their power bases undermined. The CEO said to Mike, "God, man! I needed a big whiskey after I looked at their books." (At Merrill, their CEO was saying, "When I saw their positions, my fucking knees were shaking.") Not quite the fiscal hygiene, the flushing out, Mike had in mind.

Banks drew up lists with titles like "Ten Lessons We Learned from the Hedge Fund Disaster." A so-called blue-ribbon panel, the President's Working Group on Financial Markets, found causes, suggested remedies. Congressional Banking Committee hearings were held. To date, no follow-up. Nothing. *Nada*. As if afflicted with Alzheimer's, the Fed remains adamant that banks can police themselves. Deregulation rackets along like a runaway train, banking lobbyists clinging to its side, climbing into the cab, waving from the windows, hollering in their exhilaration. *Hoo-ha.*

31

Several weeks after the hedge-fund negotiations came to an end, I was with Horace in his Town Car going uptown for a speech when his cell phone rang. The call was from the disgraced head of the hedge fund, who had invited Horace to dinner on a Friday. As he was a strict Catholic, the meat dish would be fish. Would Horace mind? When the conversation was over, Horace said, "I feel sorry for him."

"You do?"

"He lost billions. Most of it his own money."

I'd given up tugging my forelock for Horace. "I don't. He's not penniless. He'll be back in business. A question, though. Why'd you bail him out? I thought you believed in the efficiency of the markets. The markets were saying, send this hedge fund to the bottom of the ocean. And if other funds or banks join it in the briny, so be it. That's what the markets were saying."

Horace interrupted before I could expand. He hated being interrupted himself. I'd learned to wait patiently until he reached the very end of a thought, the furthermost reaches of an idea, even if I knew the conclusion. "We didn't bail him out. It was an infusion of money, an *investment*. We expect excellent returns. People forget how much money the fund made for them over the last five years." He shook his head at the fickleness of investors and returned his attention to customizing the speech he was about to give. No rattling or straining in executive Town Cars. The ride is fluffy, as if the suspension were made of beaten egg whites.

While Horace worked, I looked out the window without seeing. I would like to tell you that the Tiffany box was sitting in the middle of my mind, as difficult to banish from my consciousness as a tarantula, but it wasn't. Having made the decision, I felt empty, numb, but resolved. Instead, a Steve Earle bluegrass tune was going through my head: *I'm just a pilgrim on this road, boys/This ain't never been my home.* We were nearing our destination—an Economic Club function—when Horace put away his papers and asked, "Cath, are you okay?" He knew about Bailey. His secretaries kept him informed.

"No, I'm not okay," I blurted, startling myself. "Do you remember the retired couple down in Florida that made the news? Married more than fifty years. She had Alzheimer's. He killed her. With a shotgun. Couldn't bear it any longer. Went to jail, I think. I understand why he did it now. I understand what would drive someone to that kind of action."

Horace was alarmed, perhaps sympathetic. He tore off a piece of paper, scribbled something on it. "I want to do something for you," he said. "This is the number of a psychiatrist, a good friend of mine. Please go and see her. Tell her to send the bill to me."

Horace had his own problems. He and the CEO were at odds. Oil and water, those two. Always gentlemanly, Horace professed esteem for his colleague. The CEO was not as circumspect. Behind closed doors, he regularly referred to Horace as a horse's ass. "Horace. Horse's ass. Get it?" Most would laugh, a few wince. The problem: The CEO wanted to sell the company, cash in on the fashion for financial mega-mergers. Horace wanted Niedecker's "proud tradition" to continue.

I took the piece of paper, thanked him warmly, genuinely touched. Threw it away when I returned to my office.

32

An afterthought. It was almost an afterthought. If thinking is what I was doing; I was about to go to bed, mentally checking off the things I had needed to do to be prepared for the next day. Clothes ironed, shoes polished. And then I remembered: One more task.

I had already bought the drink. Nantucket Nectars. Orange mango. I decanted the pills from the Tiffany box into a breakfast bowl and ground them with the back of a teaspoon. I eased the powder into the drink, shook the bottle. What didn't dissolve was disguised by the sediment in the bottom.

The day passed as any in the office. Around six, I closed down my computer and caught a taxi to the home, up the FDR Drive, along the river, by the bridges. Swooping, soaring.

I chose that night because it was his bath day. He

would smell sweet, the odors of incontinence, folded flesh, rotting teeth and gut disguised by lotions, powder, soap. To bathe him, Gwen and another aide lifted him into a high plastic chair and wheeled him to the shower room. In the early days, they giggled, flirted, teased, but no longer. When I arrived, he was already in bed, his face upturned, unapprehending. I kissed him, nuzzled his hair, and then went over to nip dead leaves and spent blossoms from the geranium plants on the windowsill. More alert now, he followed my movements not with the incuriosity that had encased him these last months but approval. Or so I thought.

The time for last words, for ceremony, had passed years ago, so I got on with what I had come to do. I supported his head while he sucked at the straw. He always did have a sweet tooth.

I drew up a chair by the bed, took his hand, and read him Elizabeth Bishop's "Invitation to Miss Marianne Moore." This wasn't planned; the trip along the FDR Drive had reminded me of the poem:

From Brooklyn, over the Brooklyn Bridge, on this fine
morning,
   please come flying
In a cloud of fiery pale chemicals,
   please come flying,
to the rapid rolling of thousands of small blue drums
descending out of the mackerel sky
over the glittering grandstand of harbor-water,
   please come flying . . .

Pure joy on his face. I swear. Pure trust. Within minutes, he was asleep. Unconscious. Out of the here into the nowhere. I don't remember what I then said or did, how long I sat with him. I probably kissed him, told him how much I loved him. *This is how much I love you.* Maybe I didn't. Maybe I just walked out of the room. Goodnight to the staff on duty, down the elevator into the street. The air tasted bitter, of walnuts gone black in the shell.

The phone rang as I walked through the front door to my apartment. "Your husband is not responding. You must come." Cold, suspicious.

The medics were in his room, easing him onto a stretcher, ready to take him to the hospital I had specified. Outside were two fresh-faced policemen, caps bigger than their heads, bulky with nightsticks, walkie-talkies, guns.

"He's in the last stages of Alzheimer's," I said, looking them in the eye. They hesitated a fraction before turning on their heel and trudging away down the fluorescent-bright corridor.

He was three nights and two days dying—ample time to observe my handiwork. The skin on his face stretched tight, turned opalescent. His breathing, noisy at first, quieted. When he was moved, his eyelids shot open like a doll's. No tubes, no drips, no monitors. Propped on pillows, a cotton blanket pulled neatly under his arms. The occupant of the other bed in the room, a frail man covered in liver spots, was hooked up to all manner of machines, his family keeping an anguished vigil. Each to our own.

The first two nights, I climbed up on the bed and slept next to him, cradling him. I woke the first morning to find Gwen standing over us, horrified. Later, I asked her why, and she said she was afraid he might die in the night and I would wake to cold flesh. On the final night, his body closing down, blackening, I sat next to him, his hand in mine, sleeping fitfully. *I'm here.*

When he died in the morning, it was without even a sigh. He simply ceased to breathe.

A call was placed to the funeral parlor where I had made arrangements two years earlier, as the Medicaid law required. A no-frills cremation, as he wished, the ashes delivered to me when it was done. At the time, I asked if I could stay with the body, see it to the flames, complete the journey. But I was finally too tired. In the mortician's little van he could go the last leg alone. I went home to blistering loneliness.

33

His last conscious moments were happy. I have to remind myself of this. He was *so* happy, tucked into his bed, smiling, even then able to surround me with warmth.

He died peacefully. With dignity. How I have come to hate that word. Mingy, hollow, inadequate word. Synonym for "caused no trouble." Better to go bellowing, furious at being shortchanged.

I called the doctor who gave me the pills. "He knew! He knew!" I was hysterical.

She was a plain-spoken doctor. "Nonsense," she said. "He hasn't known anything for a very long time."

I talked with the head nun, who provided balm. She remarked on our devotion. "Cath, he never forgot who you were. That's unusual." Then she said, "It's far better this way. This could have gone on for another ten years, him lying there." Absolved?

I can't believe he's not alive. I puzzle over this lapse in comprehension, for I know he's dead. *I do believe, that die I must/And be return'd from out my dust.* Bailey has been returned from out his dust. Yet I catch myself looking around and thinking, *You have to be here somewhere*. It's as if I have a gap in my thinking that I can't bridge. Tricks of the mind. Rational brain, primitive brain.

I can't abide the sentimental scaffolding that people erect around their lives, but when I'm beset, I allow myself to talk to him, imagine what he might have said in response. He could always make me laugh at stupidity and meanness. Amateurs! he'd say, when I was upset at some piddling slight. No class! Bailey: my oracle.

Sometimes, in the spirit of Frank O'Hara, I tell him that I do not totally regret life. All the same, he asked too much of me, my darling husband.

34

Without the financial pressures presented by Bailey's care, I left Wall Street. I probably should have stayed longer, fattened my perpetually anorexic bank account, but I could no longer sit in meetings and disguise amusement, impatience, sleepiness. And, to be truthful, Bart and Hanny, with Chuck studiously looking the other way, were succeeding in aceing me by the simple trick of drying up my work. Turning off the tap. To jockey for assignments was beyond me.

When I went to Hanny to resign, he said, before I could accomplish my mission, "I'm a pretty good judge of a learning curve"—he inscribed a curve in the air with his index finger—"and you're about here." He pointed to just below the middle of the curve. "You can write, but you can't handle complex arguments."

Generous of him. "Absolutely. You're so right.

Thank you for sharing that with me. My reasoning powers definitely need developing. I'll work on it. I'll work on it very hard," I replied. Mike had taught me this trick. When someone says something preposterous, agree with them, even heighten the idiocy. For once, Hanny was flummoxed. Outside on the Hudson, a huge cruise ship—a skyscraper turned on its side—hove silently into sight. I handed him my resignation.

35

My last conversation with Horace was not in his office but in an elevator. "You know what your trouble is, Cath? You're not corporate. But underneath this"— fingering the material of his suit jacket—"neither am I." Nearly everyone at Niedecker claimed to be above the fray, going along with the absurdities of corporate life, while laughing up their sleeves. Yet they guarded their positions on the food chain with the single-mindedness, the savagery, of wolves.

I shrugged. The elevator whistled on its downward path. "Horace, working here, I've realized a funda-mental truth. Something a wise journalist once said."

"What would that be?" Cautious. Unsure where I was going with this.

"Conservatives aren't the enemy. Liberals aren't the enemy. Bullshit is the enemy."

I didn't have the last word. His faced creased with amusement. "That's my Cath." I creased my face to copy his. Every inch the court jester.

A few months later I read in the "Avenue of the Americas" column in the *Financial Times* that Horace was ousted by the CEO. *Princes come, princes go/An hour of pomp and show/They go . . .* Then—this was headline news—Niedecker Benecke was sold down the river for its good name to a large commercial bank more known for expediency and its gorilla reach than honor. Complementary synergies were invoked, but the result was a financial Pentagon: bulky, unwieldy, internecine. Niedecker could've stayed independent, but his people let him down, said the Big Toe, and, gunning his purple Porsche, drove into retirement with $250 million.

36

"A candidate for the guillotine." Mike's judgment on the Big Toe. We were lunching—Caesar salads, iced tea—in midtown at the bistro on the ground floor of the Lipstick Building. Entertaining, that building, the way its elliptical shape flirts with the surrounding rectangles. One of my favorites. It was the first time Mike and I'd had a meal together, talked anywhere other than the World Financial Center plaza.

We'd been gossiping about Niedecker, how almost everyone we knew had walked or been fired.

"It's a carcass," he said.

I agreed. "Poor buggers. They didn't know what hit them." We talked about the fates of ex-colleagues for a while, and then I said, "Enough of them. What are *you* going to do now?"

"Right. Yeah. Been wrestling with that one. I've had

job offers, good ones. With some start-up boutique banks. The future *has* to lie with them. The center won't hold at the giants. Clients will get fed up. But I can't go back into harness. I stayed too long as it was. If anyone should've known that the dice were loaded, it was me. If you think about it, what the banks ideally want is the conditions in Russia. No regulatory bodies, a financial Wild West. You'd think that . . ."

He was off and running. I'd heard it all before. I interrupted. "Mike, what are you going to do?"

"I'm selling up, going south. To Costa Rica. I bought a dive school."

I tried to picture Mike, all arms and legs, as a scuba diver. He must have read my thoughts. "I'm one of those people who are happier in water than on land." Okay. Not the first to come to finance via Marx, not the last to wind up owning a dive school. Or a fishing boat. Or a bait shop. Chasing a delinquent crouton around his plate, he turned the conversation toward me. "Tell me, Cath, what did you learn in the last six years?"

"You mean, what was my 'take-away'?" Rolling my eyes.

"If you want to put it that way, yeah."

"We're rather keen in this country on learning lessons, as if everything were a test and not just life happening. No pain, no gain—all that bunkum. I could do without the pain, thank you."

"Cath . . ."

"I interrupted you, I know, but let me finish. Big on learning lessons, on self-improvement. Reinvention! And let's not forget closure. Closure this, closure that. Everything tied up with a neat bow. What if you don't learn anything? What if you just put one foot in front of the other? Sure, I've changed. I'm older. I'm on the other side of fifty, unable to see the point in anything, and lonely as all hell. Try tying that into a neat bow." Gabbling. Too much information. I stopped, cleared my throat. "Actually, I did learn something. The dailiness of life—that's what gets you through hard times. Putting on your pantyhose, eating breakfast, catching the subway. That's what stops your heart from breaking."

Mike looked embarrassed. "I didn't mean your personal life. I meant Wall Street. What's your opinion of that now?"

"Oh. Okay." I regained my composure. "Did you see the cartoon last week in the *Financial Times*? A banker is saying to one of those determined spinster types—hair in a bun, handbag in her lap—'You're a shrewd woman, Miss Jones. I'll put my hands up now and admit we merchant bankers are, in fact, in it for the money.'" He laughed. "And you, Mike, what's your take-away? What did you learn?"

He didn't hestitate. "Pierpont Morgan said—at least I think he said it—that the only thing you can be certain about on Wall Street is that stocks will go up, stocks will go down. So that's it, I guess. The markets will continue as always, stocks going up and down. Yield curves steepening or flattening. Spreads narrowing or widening." He slowly let out an indrawn breath. "But you can be certain of something else. Someone, somewhere, sooner rather than later, will take on absurdly high levels of leverage and make a bad bet based on a model created by fallible human beings. And then fingers will be pointed, heads roll. A firm will disappear or a government fall." He shrugged. "Or not."

I chimed in. "And corporations like Niedecker will do good. And bad. Jargon will be used, process engineered. Middle managers—the Chucks, Hannys, Barts—will flatter and elbow, multiply and prosper, as they always have. Golf will be played, bonuses given. And you know what? I don't really care. I wish I cared more, but I don't."

"Chuck is not middle management."

"You get my gist. Strange thing, though. I hated every moment while I was there, but I'm not sorry for the experience."

"Glad to hear it."

"We're a sanguine pair, aren't we?"

The waiter stopped by to ask if we wanted dessert. We shook our heads.

Mike caught my gaze, held it. "Cath, you talked to Horace, didn't you? You told him what I knew about the hedge fund. Implied that I wasn't doing anything about it."

"I did. I'm deeply sorry."

"It's okay. 'Name me someone that's not a parasite/ And I'll go out and say a prayer for him.' Bob Dylan."

"'Visions of Johanna.'"

"They would have fired me, anyway."

"It would seem that way, given what happened to other risk managers." I clambered back to safer ground. "Quoting Bob Dylan now? What's happening? Changing your allegiance from Leonard to Bobby?"

"Nah. Leonard will always have first place in my heart. My main man."

Mike took the bill when it came. I protested, he insisted. "Well, thank you. That was delightful," I said. "And thanks for your company over these last years. Our chats—they meant a lot to me. To be honest, at the beginning—and I'm sure you knew this—I could barely tell a stock from a bond. Balancing my checkbook was beyond me, much less understanding option pricing trees. You were very patient. For me, it was like having the dark side of the moon illuminated."

Mike closed the plastic folder on the Amex receipt, put his pen away in his inside pocket. "My pleasure. On both counts." he said.

"Still can't balance my checkbook," I said.

Out on the pavement, we said our good-byes. Pecks on both cheeks, followed by a quick, small hug. Mike was heading downtown to Grand Central, I uptown. I had gone a few paces when I turned to watch his progress. Mike walked as if pushing into the future: his upper body angled forward, eyes on the ground. He felt in his pocket for something. Probably gum. He mentioned he was giving up smoking.

I remember once watching Bailey unobserved. We

were over near Barney's and had parted company, I to shop, he to an appointment at a Fifty-seventh Street art gallery. He always said that every block in New York was a movie, and that's how he behaved, eyes busy, happily curious, soaking it all up, oblivious to his portfolio slapping at his leg. There was always something of the small boy about Bailey. Eager, transparent, unafraid. A bursting boy. Look, Ma, the *world*.

Author's Note

For readers unfamiliar with finance and wanting to know more about the subject than a short novel can bear, I recommend Martin Mayer's *The Bankers* and *The Fed*, James Buchan's *Frozen Desire*, Roger Lowenstein's *When Genius Failed*, and Nicholas Dunbar's *Inventing Money*. Of course, the views expressed in *Moral Hazard* are those of my characters.

Acknowledgments